OCTOGENARIAN
SLEUTH

— THE CASE OF —

THE

Queen's

DIAMOND
BROOCH

by Bill Petersen

The Octogenarian Sleuth—A Sequel

THE QUEEN'S DIAMOND BROOCH

by Bill Petersen
The Octogenarian Sleuth—Fourth in the Series

Copyright @ 2014

This book is a work of fiction. Names of actual people and places are used, but the depictions are products of the author's imagination and are used fictitiously. Any resemblance to actual events or of characterizations of persons living or dead is entirely coincidental. And thanks to all for taking the fictional insults with good humor.

Design and cover by Elizabeth Petersheim
Idea by Tom Dulaney,
Editing by Randy Petersen

Library of Congress Number: 2014919045
International Standard Book Number: 978-1-60126-438-1

Printed 2014 by
Masthof Press
219 Mill Road
Morgantown, PA 19543-9516

THE Queen's DIAMOND BROOCH

If you're writing a trilogy, I think you should stop with three. No one would be interested in a four-book trilogy, would they?

That's what I thought too.

But my editor disagreed.

I said I was devoid of ideas; I couldn't write a fourth book for a trilogy.

He said, "That doesn't matter. Famous novelists aren't dependent on fresh ideas. The most successful novelists use stale ideas all the time. I can list a dozen for you if you will listen."

"OK, I believe you, but I'm an octogenarian author writing about an octogenarian sleuth and I am tired and the sleuth is tired and we have solved all the crimes worth solving."

"You like to travel, don't you?"

"Sure, I used to, when I could."

"And you liked to visit England, didn't you?."

"Of course I did. But I don't like to travel alone anymore."

"That's why you have an assistant named Samantha."

"But Samantha has a husband."

"Maybe she could bring her husband along with her, and if he doesn't want to come, have her bring along her mother. And maybe the Queen of England, who also happens to be an octogenarian, has a problem that only an octogenarian detective can solve."

"Oh, come on, that's unbelievable."

"Aren't all your stories unbelievable?".

I felt trapped. When you're an octogenarian, you can easily get confused on what actually happened and what is just a figment of your imagination. So hang on for the ride!

CHAPTER 1

It was unbelievable how it happened. You see, lately I had been reading the classic detective stories of Sherlock Holmes and imagining what it might have been like to work with Sherlock, when—and this is the unbelievable part—I got an email from London, from a gentleman named John H. Watson IV.

I didn't know anyone named Watson in London. Of course, I was acquainted with Sherlock's sidekick, Dr. Watson, and I knew both Holmes and Watson were fictional characters made up from the fanciful imagination of Sir Arthur Conan Doyle. But as far as a real Dr. Watson, living today in London? No way. I wouldn't have known him from Adam—probably from Eve, but not from Adam.

Here's all the e-mail said: "If you are still taking criminal cases, phone me John H. Watson IV collect at 1-44-207-301-9202. I need to hear from you immediately if not sooner."

I don't know if he was trying to impress me or not, but adding IV in Roman numerals didn't do it. Now if he had said he was Louis XVIII of France I might have been impressed.

And I didn't like the way he worded it: "If you are still taking criminal cases." Was he implying that I was too old to solve a problem? Did he think I was senile? Just because I didn't put a full-page ad in *The Wall Street Journal* didn't mean I was no longer detectiving or sleuthing

Yes, Watson IV had a fancy moniker; but so did I. I was Pete Petersen I. And besides that, sixty years ago when I was drafted into military service, I was selected for a military police battalion, no doubt because of my superior IQ and my outstanding physique. After six or eight weeks of intensive basic training as an MP, I was transferred into another company because of my outstanding typing skills close to 30 words a minute without error and before Spellcheck. In this elite company I was entrusted with top secret information, according to my master sergeant; my keen memory has retained all that was vital to national security for the past sixty years. Now, as the internationally famous octogenarian sleuth, I have been solving crimes that have been mind-boggling to the major law enforcement agencies of the nation, well, at least to some of the police in Colorado Springs. I say this in true humility, as long as Samantha isn't around.

My partner in crime-fighting, in case you have forgotten, is the lovely aforementioned Samantha, sixty years my junior, who has completed a two-year college program in criminal justice and crime scene investigation. Anything that developed during the sixty-year hiatus between my glory days as an Army military policeman and today, Samantha can fill in. Besides that, she moves more quickly, thinks faster, drives her yellow Beetle more recklessly, and has up-to-date contacts with the FBI and CIA. You know, little details like that. And most people would probably say she is prettier than I am, though I have had time to survey only five men on that.

I forgot to say that I am a man of action, so having received this email, I knew I needed to formulate a plan post-haste.

Yes, I was a man of action and I was also organized, but, humble as I am, I didn't want to make my organizational abilities too obvious. Some folks might actually think I am messy, but that's because they only know the external me. The internal me is very neat and organized.

I was curious about Watson IV. I was also curious about Watson III, and Watson Jr., but they could wait their turn.

And I was curious about that thirteen- or was it fourteen-digit telephone number. Having a number with that many digits is almost obscene. Since he asked me to call him collect, I thought I might do it just for the experience. After all, you don't call fourteen-digit telephone numbers every day; at least I don't.

I imagined what would happen when I phoned. Someone would pick up the phone after nine or ten rings, and I would be asked for Watson IV's extension, and that would be another two or three digits, bringing the grand total to sixteen or seventeen. (How does mortal man remember all of that?) Sometime during the process I would be placed on hold, while they played recorded Muzak music for a half hour or whatever they played in the British Isles. Maybe there they would play "God Save the Queen" for a half hour.

I was getting riled up before I even placed the call.

It also bothered me that Watson IV, or whatever his real name was, needed to hear from me "immediately if not sooner." Just to show him that I was a busy man, I decided to wait another ten minutes before responding. During those ten minutes, I would do two things:

First, I needed to ask our receptionist at the front desk where Watson IV might be located. With a name like Watson IV, he was probably in England, although he might be vacationing in the South Pacific. From all those numbers our receptionist should be able to tell me if Watson IV lived in a little grass shack in Tahiti or if he was listening to an old Beatles recording in Liverpool.

Second, I needed to phone Samantha and find out if she was at all interested in visiting either one of those places.

Now to put the plan into action.

I printed out the email and showed it to the receptionist. "This may take you a half-hour, but I would like to know . . ."

Before I finished the sentence, she said, "It's from London, England. Anything else you need to know, Pete?"

"Of course," I said, "but London is a big city. What part of London?" She wasn't going to get away with a flip answer like that.

"I don't know exactly, but the 207 says that it comes from the inner city." She sounded a bit humbler now, because she admitted she didn't know everything. "Do you want me to place the call for you now?"

"No, not yet." I needed to remember what Action Step 2 was. So I told her, "I'll be getting back to you in a few minutes." I thought it would serve Watson IV right to have my receptionist place the call instead of me placing the call. Now I needed to call Samantha next. And besides that, I had other important things to do, although I couldn't remember what they were at the moment. But in a retirement community like this, a resident has many demands on his time: bingo games, bridge games, and educational lectures on major issues like *Was James Polk a better President than Chester A. Arthur?* All of those matters take precedence over talking to someone in the inner city of London, England, although it's possible he might be Chancellor of the Exchequer or the Checkers Champ of Chichester-on-Chelsey, or whatever else Watson IV might claim to be.

So number 2 on my list was to call Samantha. Considering the fact that she never had the military police training that I had sixty years ago, she was still a bright young lady. Her antenna was always up. In a couple previous cases, I had been beguiled by beautiful women, but Samantha sensed the problem before I did. I doubted if Watson IV was a beautiful woman, but you never can be sure about anything in detective work.

So I phoned Samantha and got her answering machine. At least she didn't have Muzak playing on it or "God Save the Queen."

Sometimes I hate answering machines, but usually I wish I had one. My guess is that Watson IV's answering machine would probably greet me by saying, "I am sorry, old chap, but I am frightfully engaged at the moment, so if it isn't too much of an inconvenience to you, I would be forever grateful if you would patiently forbear for a few moments, and if you can't forbear, cheerio, bully for you, and keep a stiff upper lip, remembering what Sir Winston Churchill said, 'There is nothing to fear except the present and the future.'"

I had just finished telling Samantha's answering machine who I was, when I heard Samantha's voice. "Hi, Pete, what's up?"

Maybe I shouldn't allow a young woman to talk so flippantly to me, but after someone has saved your life a couple times, you let her get away with a few things, and, besides, I sort of liked her.

"Do you know anyone named Watson IV?"

"Male or female?" Samantha was good at asking perceptive questions like that.

"First name John."

"Sounds like a male." She was also good at drawing quick deductions.

"That's what I thought. So I will give him a jingle on the telly and find what it's all about."

"A jingle on the telly? What are you talking about, Pete?"

'Oh, didn't I tell you? Watson IV is calling from London, England, I think. I'll keep you informed. But oh, if it amounts to anything, would you rather go to Tahiti or Liverpool?" And, having said that, I hung up the phone because Watson IV wanted me to respond "immediately if not sooner."

Then some chimes started ringing in my brain. Octogenarians, you know, have brains with voluminous storage capacity. It isn't the storage capacity that is the problem. The problem is that the retrieval technology hasn't kept up.

It bothered me that I couldn't track down John H. Watson IV in my memory warehouse. The name was somewhat familiar. Then in my usual perspicacious manner, I broke the name down. Maybe I knew the grandfather of Watson IV. Maybe it was John Watson, who was a great cricketeer. No, that wasn't John Watson; the cricketeer was Jiminy Watson. Who was the Watson I knew from London? Maybe it would come to me as our receptionist was making the transatlantic phone call and as I was listening to a recording of "God Save the Queen" while Watson IV was playing on the floor with Watson V.

And then suddenly the light went on. Watson IV was a fraud.

I wasted no more time. I asked the receptionist to place the call for me, and to be sure to make it collect.

I thought I might take a short nap while waiting to get through all the digits on Watson IV's phone number. But I didn't. I had just gotten my notepad in front of me, and I didn't even have a chance to kick off my shoes before my phone rang.

"Mr. Petersen, I have the Honorable Mr. John H. Watson IV on the line." I was glad that she didn't call me Pete when she was calling him the Honorable Mr.

But my strategy didn't change; I needed to put him on the defense immediately.

"Hi, Mr. Watson IV. I know who you are. You are a fraud, a fig newton of Arthur Conan Doyle's imagination."

"Good afternoon, sir. I think you mean a figment, not a fig newton.

"Whatever. But figments and fig newtons both come from Britain."

"No, I beg to differ with you, Dr. Petersen, but fig newtons are cookies developed in Newton, Massachusetts, and figments are derived from the Latin *figmentum* meaning fiction, so we cannot take credit for either of those things. But, Dr. Petersen, I must compliment you on your insight, because in one sense I am a figment, as you say, although in another sense I am not."

"Thank you for the compliment." He called me Doctor, and that made me forget what else he said. Willing to let bygones be bygones, I liked that too, because I had a lot of bygones, probably more than most people. So I continued,

"And now Mr. Watson IV, what can I do for you?"

"All right, old chap, let's put all our cards on the table."

"OK," I replied. I hoped he was playing with a full deck, because I didn't see any table.

"Here's the story of my life in two minutes."

I looked at my watch and decided to time him.

"My name really is John H. Watson IV, but obviously no relation to the fictional Watson that Sir Arthur Conan Doyle created for his Sherlock Holmes stories. I studied at Oxford just as my father and grandfather did. I majored in modern English Literature and I specialized in the nineteenth-century writers."

"Ah, yes," I knew my nineteenth-century British authors too. "You mean writers like Dickens and Robert Louis Stevenson."

"Yes, and Hardy, Scott, Bronte, Kipling, Stoker, Austen, H.G. Wells, Conrad, and Lewis Carroll."

"You didn't mention Arthur Conan Doyle."

"No, I didn't, because I didn't consider him in the top tier of British authors. But in 1988 on the 100th anniversary of Doyle's classic *Study in Scarlet*, I was asked to write an assessment of it for a British publication. Because I was examining it from a literary point of view, I had to explain that I was not related to the fictional Dr. John Watson, who was the assistant for Sherlock Holmes."

"Your two minutes are up, but it doesn't explain why you are calling me. Long distance."

"Well, Dr. Petersen, after that article appeared, I was contacted by the Sherlock Holmes Museum to give a lecture on Conan Doyle and Sherlock Holmes at the museum. They thought it might be good PR, as you say across the pond in America, to have a real John Watson talk about the fictional Sherlock Holmes. It proved to be so successful that they offered me a room above the museum, and since I was retiring from the academic world, I took it, and it has been my home ever since, in exchange for a few lectures on the subject."

I still hadn't gotten a satisfactory answer on why he was phoning me; I knew his phone bill was increasing faster than a cabbie's meter, so I decided to move along the conversation.

"But Dr. Watson IV, what does all of that have to do with me?"

"I was getting to that, if you will hold your horses."

"I have been holding my horses for five minutes."

"Good, and when I tell you that the Queen will be sending you 20,000 dollars to solve a mystery, you will be glad to hold your horses for five more minutes."

"Twenty thousand dollars?" This guy had to be full of baloney, or whatever the Brits were using for lunch meat these days.

But I would hear him out.

"Can I call you Pete?"

"For 20,000 dollars you can call me anything?"

"Well, Pete, you probably know that the first person to use the expression, 'Hold your horses,' or something close to that, was Homer in the *Iliad,* more than two thousand years ago. However, the phrase became popular in the 1840s as the American pioneers started moving westward by covered wagons, and they tended to pronounce it, 'Hold yor' hosses.'"

"Yes, yes. John, if I may call you that." Couldn't this guy ever get to the point? "What about this 20,000 dollars from the Queen?"

"Did I say 20,000 dollars? I meant 20,000 pounds."

"What's the difference?"

'It varies day to day, but as of today 20 thousand pounds would equal about 30,000 dollars."

"It still seems like thirty thousand fig newtons to me. I guess I don't understand what the Queen has to do with it."

"Queen Elizabeth is a dedicated monarch; she loves being the Queen, and she loves her family, but she also has four other loves—you might call them extracurricular loves. She loves her dogs, her horses, her crossword puzzles and her mystery stories, and I don't know in what order. Sometimes, I think more than anything else she loves to read mystery stories. Two or three times a year I receive a phone call from her about a mystery she has read. Why me? Because she trusts me and she trusts the Sherlock Holmes Museum. She knows I won't say anything to Rupert Murdoch and the press about the latest mystery she has been reading.

And Pete, you must promise not to say anything to anyone about this royal assignment either. If you do, it's all off."

"I don't even know if it's 'on' yet. And I don't know what's 'royal' about it? What royal assignment?"

"I don't know, Pete. It's a mystery to me too. But I can tell you what I know."

"Nothing makes sense to me yet, John, so you have to tell me more. And go slowly;   I'm an octogenarian, you know."

"And I'm not far behind you as a septuagenarian. All right, here is all I know. The Queen has read a couple of your mysteries; she printed them out from the internet. She liked them and she even gave one of them to her husband, Prince Philip, who seldom reads fiction, and he loved it."

"Go on," He was starting to make sense. My left ear was getting tired so I switched the phone to my right ear.

"All right. A week ago I got a phone call summoning me to a private meeting with the Queen. This is extremely unusual. The Queen has often phoned me about a mystery story she was reading, but only once before had I talked with her in person."

I could imagine the conversation. "Hello, John IV. This is Elizabeth II. I have just read Shakespeare's Macbeth I for the seventeenth (XVIIth) time, and I still don't think he killed King Duncan." And then John IV might have said, "Excuse me, your Majesty, but Lady Macbeth seemed certain of it." "I know that, John IV, but you must remember that Lady Macbeth was daft."

John IV continued talking. The way he droned tended to put me to sleep. "So I had my appointment with Her Majesty, and she told me that she had read all your books, and she thought it would be advisable to enlist your help in solving a personal problem she had. And this is it. She has lost something quite valuable. It might have been a theft, or it might just have been something she lost in one of her travels. Anyway, they have kept it discreetly out of the press. She said she would explain it further when you came."

It still sounded fishy to me. "Why doesn't she just go to Scotland Yard about it?" I asked. I mean, if you have a whole bunch of detectives in your back yard, that should be your first option, I would think.

"I asked her that," he replied, as if expecting the question. "While she trusts Scotland Yard in solving cases, she doesn't trust the Yard in keeping royal secrets. Sooner or later the details of the theft would come out, she feared. Apparently the Queen has had some bad experiences with the Yard that way. She needs secrecy, and secrecy would best be assured by someone outside the country; she thought an American would be advisable, an American not involved with the CIA or FBI, and then she asked if I knew you. I said that I didn't know you but that I was certain I could locate you. She said, 'Do it as soon as possible. The Keeper of the Privy Purse will send the necessary funds to your museum and you can disburse them to the American detectives.' And, honestly, love, that is all I know about it."

My mind was going lickety-split, and all of a sudden it stopped. I don't know if Watson IV could hear it go lickety-split, or maybe he heard a thud when it stopped. Anyway, after thirty seconds of silence, he asked, "Are you there, love, are you there?"

"Yes, I am here, I am here." I knew the Brits called everybody "love," but it bothered me, and then I wasn't ready to give an answer on the spur of the moment, partly because I began wondering why moments had spurs.

"And what is your answer, Dr. Petersen? You will come to London, won't you?"

"I'm thinking, I'm thinking."

"In one of your books you said that octogenarian sleuths liked challenges, and that no case was too difficult for Pete and Samantha."

"Did I write that? Maybe that was another fig newton of my imagination." For all I knew, he might have been making that up.

"You wrote that, Pete. And you can't let her Royal Highness down. She probably read that too. So she is counting on you. Can I tell the Queen's private secretary to pass the word along to her Majesty that you have accepted the challenge?"

"How long will she give us to solve the case, whatever it is?"

"I don't know, Pete, but the Queen likes things to happen quickly, and she gets impatient easily. So my guess is that the Queen would like the case, whatever it is, to be solved in a week, and no more than ten days."

"And you don't have the slightest idea what the crime was— if there was a crime?"

"No, not the slightest idea. I will wire the money to you immediately. As soon as you give me the address of your bank, we will deposit the funds directly to your account."

Had I really agreed to anything yet or was he just assuming that I couldn't turn him down? Maybe if I put up enough roadblocks, he would have second thoughts about our availability. So I said, "You know, of course, that we will require accommodations, and accommodations in London are not cheap."

"Yes, I realize that. The best way to keep this low key is to have you stay at the museum. Rooms on our upper floors are available for special guests."

"And do you have an elevator for octogenarians?" That should stop him.

"Yes, we do. In fact, they put the lift in when I began living here. You see, I use a cane."

I thought that all Englishmen over forty used canes. "And if we are not successful, will the Queen put us in the Tower of London?"

Watson IV laughed. "No, Pete, you don't have to be afraid of that. But I didn't think that you and Samantha were ever unsuccessful."

"I'll talk to Samantha and call you back tomorrow."

"Hunky-dory, love."

Hunky-dory, love? I was glad Samantha would be going with me. Maybe she could translate phrases like that.

CHAPTER 2

A good detective is trained to be suspicious, and I was suspicious of Watson IV from the get-go. I felt he was pressuring me into a hasty agreement, but I wasn't as gullible as he thought. He would have to show me the money first. He said he would wire the money directly to my bank as soon as he had the bank address and my account number.

And my account number? That gave it away.

It was a clever variation of the old Nigerian email scam. I was sure of it. In the traditional scam, a widow in Lagos, Nigeria, has inherited millions of dollars and now wants to find a safe haven for it in America. All she needs is your bank account number and she will wire the money directly to your account. She plans to come to America next summer and will divvy up the money with you fifty-fifty. The scam, of course, is when that "widow" gets your bank number, she will clear your life-long savings from your account.

These scam artists prey on us octogenarians. They must think that most of us are filthy rich and gullible. But not me. I may be filthy, but not rich and gullible.

The more I thought about it, the more convinced I became that Watson IV was not only a fraud but also a scam artist. He had developed a Piccadilly variation of the Lagos scam. The Brits probably knew him already as Jack the Rip-off.

But I could trap him easily. I knew I could.

Last week my bank had notified me of a joint checking account I once had with my late wife who died several years ago. I hadn't written a check on the account since a month after she had passed away, and the balance was only $7.67. To tell the truth, I had forgotten about it.

I decided to give Jack the Rip-off that bank account number. I might lose seven dollars, but then Scotland Yard should be able to track him down before he spent it all in Monte Carlo.

So I emailed Watson IV the joint checking account number, and then not wasting any time I phoned Molly, the bank teller who always made sure my Social

Security checks were deposited properly. She was the person at the bank who knew me best and could keep track of any unusual withdrawals from my accounts.

"Molly, this is Pete. I have a— Pete *Petersen*. You told me once that I was your favorite depositor. Well, there's a— My date of birth? Well, that was a long time ago."

I gave it to her, and she said, "*Now* I remember. That's the same date of birth you gave me last time."

"Well, Molly, I need to ask a favor from you. In the next twenty minutes a major withdrawal might be made from my inactive account, but probably not. Understand? And I will be calling you back later to see what happened. OK? Got that straight?"

"Yes," she said cheerily. "I mean, no. What was that again?"

I tried to explain the details of the brilliant trap I was setting for Jack the Rip-off IV. She couldn't get past the fact that it was an inactive account. "I think we would have to activate it first."

"Then let's do that right away," I ordered, worried that precious seconds were ticking away.

"Ooooh, that's not so easy, Mr. Petersen. I think we have to get some signatures on that."

"Any particular signatures?" I asked. I remember getting an autographed baseball from a Yankee second baseman years ago. Maybe they would accept that.

"*Your* signature of course," she giggled. "And probably my supervisor's. This is all getting pretty complicated, Mr. Petersen. Maybe you should stop by here and explain it in person. If you still drive. Have a nice day."

"But, Molly. . ." The line was dead. I was sure that Molly hadn't hung up on me. It must have been one of those new receptionists.

If I still drive . . . ? How could I be the famous octogenarian sleuth if I couldn't drive a car? Of course, Samantha always drives when we're on a case, but I could if I needed to. And besides, the bank was only a quarter-mile away from the retirement community. I could get there in . . . well, within the hour, I'm sure.

First I needed to call Samantha and let her know that the email I received from Watson IV was a false alarm, a Piccadilly scam or something like that.

It was preposterous from the start. So I phoned her:

"Samantha?"

"Hi, Pete, I'm getting excited already."

"About what?"

"About going to London."

"But I said it was just a *possibility.*"

"I know, Pete, but I decided that it would be best if my husband didn't go with us. He needs to stay home with the kids and to make some money so I can afford to do some shopping. But my Mom adores London, and she mentioned a store named Harrod's which has everything, and she has her passport and would be ready to go in twenty-four hours. And I have my passport too; I got it when my husband and I thought we might honeymoon in Hawaii."

I hated to interrupt her but I had to. "Samantha, you don't need a passport to go to Hawaii."

"Yeah, Pete, I know that *now*. In fact, I found that out in Honolulu. But we do need one for England. Do you have yours yet?"

"Well, I think so, but I'm not sure." She did this all the time. I would be taking the offensive, and all of a sudden I found I was playing defense. But now, I needed to break through her false enthusiasm and burst her bubble. She could solve murders and deal with the Mafia and al Qaeda without too much excitement, but now I had to tell her that Watson IV was trying to bilk me, and that London was off the radar. "Samantha, Samantha," I called into the phone to get her attention.

"Yes, Pete."

"I'm not sure there will be a trip to London."

"Then Liverpool or Tahiti? You mentioned the possibility of all three."

"All I said was that I had gotten an email from someplace like that."

"But why were you phoning me if there wasn't an actual case involved?"

I heard a beep as she asked her question, and that meant someone was trying to phone me. It had to be Molly at the bank.

"Samantha, I'll explain later. Right now, I have an important person trying to reach me on another line."

I never quite figured out how to answer one call while being on another, and by the time I get out of the call I'm on, the new caller is usually long gone. It had to be Molly, and I was headed to the bank in person, so I would just talk with her there. The receptionist flagged me down on the way past her desk. "Is everything all right, Pete? You never picked up that call."

"Oh, yes, just very busy." I decided not to divulge my difficulty with call waiting.

"It was Mr. Watson, your friend from England."

My friend from England? I didn't trust the guy. No doubt he was sweet-talking the receptionist to get a new angle on me. Not only a fraud and a scam artist, he might also be a spy, and I wasn't going to let him make a fool out of me. I don't like it when people take advantage of senior citizens.

"He said I should tell you *the transfer has been made*." She took on a hushed tone in delivering the message.

"The transfer? What on earth was he—? Oh." That guy was working fast. I muttered to the receptionist, "Well, I'll have to call him later. I'm going to the bank."

I probably shouldn't have said that about the bank. With all this talk of "transfers" and "banks," she would probably assume I was wangling some high-finance deals, when I was just trying to avoid getting ripped off by her new pal Watson. What to do about Samantha was another problem. She sounded as if she and her mother had their bags packed. Both of them would be very disappointed when I told them it was all a scam.

My head was spinning. Too much was happening. One thing at a time, Pete, I told myself, one at a time. First, I had to straighten things out with my old friend Molly. So I drove the quarter-mile to the bank and ambled in with my old joint account number, my driver's license, and my social security number. I also brought an old class picture from the third grade, in case that would help. Molly was on a coffee break and her supervisor was filling in for her, so I tactfully decided to wait until Molly got back. I didn't want to have to explain everything all over again to that supervisor. Besides, she looked mean.

You would think that waiting would come easier for senior citizens; after all, practice makes perfect, but I don't think that applies to waiting.

Eventually, Molly returned to her usual perch. "Welcome to First National. How can I help you, sir?" Molly's supervisor was standing right behind her. Molly gave me half a smile, which looked like it could have been a wink.

I nodded to show that I understood the situation.

"Thank you, Miss," I said as politely as I could. With the supervisor there, I wanted to be on my best behavior. "If it wouldn't be too much of an imposition, ma'am, I would like to reactivate this account." I showed her the old checkbook with the old account number on it.

"No problem, sir. But I will need to have some identification."

"Of course, and I happen to have those things with me. I remember when I entered kindergarten, my mother reminded me to carry my date of birth, my social security number and my driver's license with me at all times." I tried to wink back at Molly without her supervisor seeing, but it ended up like more of a tic. When the "super" glared back at me, I made a mental note never to wink at a bank teller again.

Molly pulled out a form for me to sign, and she slid it over to her supervisor, who signed it with sort of a harrumph. "That's all we need," said Molly sweetly. "That wasn't so bad now, was it?"

"Now I'm also wondering," I added, "if there's been any attempted activity in this account over the last hour or so."

"No problem," the teller responded, punching a couple of buttons on her computer. A printer spat out a thin strip of paper, which she gave to me.

I looked at it, nodded, and said, "Just as I suspected." There was no activity on the account—no deposits, no withdrawals. My $7.67 was still safely there. If Watson IV had designs on it, he was probably waiting until after dark to do his dirty work.

I turned away, but Molly said, "Wait, Pete. Let me check one other thing. It might be in the system but not entered to your account yet." She left for a back room.

The supervisor was shaking her head. Molly was going to too much trouble for a run-of-the mill customer like me. Gruffly, the woman stepped up to Molly's perch and waved me aside to wait on the next person in line.

Five minutes later, Molly returned with a smile. "It was in the system, but because it came from another country, it took longer to be processed into your account." She handed me a new computer printout.

I looked at it in disbelief. My $7.67 was still there, but now it had some digits in front of it, for a total of $29,007.67.

If I hadn't found a bench they might have had to scrape me up from the marble floor. Maybe Watson IV wasn't a fraud after all. I fished a 3 x 5 card in my pocket to write on. I had to develop a new game plan now.

A. Phone Watson IV, collect, of course.

B. Phone Samantha. The trip was on.

C. See if my passport was still valid.

No, strike that. I should check on my passport first. Why? Two reasons.

1. To see if I could find it. Since moving into this retirement community, I had no reason to use it; I was sure I didn't throw it

out when downsizing for the sixth time.

    2. If and when I found it, I needed to make sure it hadn't expired.

    No, strike that again. (It's amazing how much info you can squeeze onto a 3 x 5 card if you write small enough.) I should look for the passport last, because even though I had only 1,200 square feet in my apartment, it might take me eight hours to find it. Watson IV was reinstated in first position again.

    As soon as I got back to my apartment, I asked the receptionist to place the call to my old pal Watson IV, and I also asked her if she remembered his first name.

    She told me, and when I opened the door to my room my phone was ringing. I picked it up and the receptionist said: "The Honorable *John* Watson IV is on the line."

    "John, old friend, old matey, love, how are you?" It's always good to throw in a few Britishisms to let them know you are communicating.

    "The money? Oh, yes, it arrived at my bank just as you said it would. I never worried about that one second. You said it was coming and your word is good as gold for me." I wasn't sure whether Britain was on the gold standard.

    His voice wasn't coming through as clearly as it had the last time. At times it faded in the middle of a sentence so it was hard to understand him.

    "You say that the Queen's secretary phoned you and wondered when we would be arriving? Well, I was just talking to Samantha about that earlier today, and she is just as eager to tackle the assignment as I am. We'll be booking our flights as soon as we can. Incidentally, it will be Samantha and her mother Shirley, plus me, of course."

    He reminded me again that this was top secret, and that no

one, not even Samantha's mother, should know that our confidential mission involved Queen Elizabeth herself. I assured him that we had handled secret missions before, and I also reminded him that I had security clearance from the U.S. government, although I didn't say that my security clearance was sixty years old.

Once again he urged me to move quickly, and as soon as I had the flights scheduled, I should call him again.

"Yes, John, I will give you the information on our arrival time in London as soon as we book our flights."

"Right-o, love; we'll be talking again soon."

I decided to wait until after dinner to talk to Samantha. She would be serving tables again, and as soon as the tables were cleared, she would have some time to talk. But next, my passport, which had now become (B) instead of (C), although I couldn't read my 3 x 5 card any more.

I had developed a new system for finding lost items in my apartment. I don't know if I could get a patent or a copyright on it, but it had worked for me four out of seven times. And it was simple.

All I needed to do was write down the five least likely places for the lost item to be found, and invariably I would locate it in one of those five, although I have to admit that four out of seven does not equal "invariably." But you have to agree that it is twice as good as two out of seven.

Anyway, my current list of least likely places to find my passport included the wastebaskets, the washer and dryer, the microwave, the refrigerator and the oven.

My desk and the pockets of my suitcoats were too obvious. Another too-obvious location would be in my bookcase stashed between books on Afghanistan and Zimbabwe, but I tended to loan my books out for indefinite periods, and who knows how many people would be interested in finding out all there is to know about Zimbabwe?

No, even as I made out my list I knew it was in the refrigerator, tucked away neatly behind the A-1 sauce which I never use and my special Greek sauce for gyro sandwiches, which I bought five years ago and was reserved for all my Greek friends. I didn't have any Greek friends at the moment; I thought a new resident might be Greek and was disappointed to find out that she was from Herzegovina instead. There was an expiration date on the bottle, but I tore it off because I didn't think Greeks paid any attention to expiration dates. If it was good enough for Sophocles, it should be good enough for me and any Greek friends I might have in the future.

And what did I tell you? My passport was stuck on the back of the A-1 sauce, because some careless user, probably my daughter when she came over last summer or the summer before that, had not tightened the cap properly. But—who knows?—a little A-1 sauce on a passport might help me get through customs more rapidly.

On opening the passport, which wasn't easy for obvious reasons, I noted that the expiration date was only seven months away. The passport's expiration, not mine. So I made a mental note to have the passport renewed in case the Sultan of South Sudan or the Grand Duke of Kazakhstan requested our services after we returned from seeing Queen Elizabeth II. The only problem with being on a secret mission, of course, was that you can't use it on your résumé, if we had a résumé.

When I found my passport, it was too late to phone Samantha. She was probably upstairs in the dining room setting tables by now. So I decided to write her a cryptic note on a sticky Post-it and attach it to my empty soup dish, which she would read as she hurried back to the kitchen. Samantha moved so quickly at suppertime that it was hard to communicate with her unless you slapped a sticky note on her wrist or on a dirty dish as she flitted by.

When I ran out of Post-its or missed as I tried to slap it on her wrist, I would send her an email and she would reply by texting me. At first, texting was like a foreign language to me, but gradually I picked it up. Tonight, because there wasn't much space on a Post-it to write a longer message, I decided to show her how well I was doing with my texting lingo. So on my Post-it, I wrote, "CU@7:45 YDOK? IT'S A GO!" and stuck it on the side of my empty soup dish.

A minute later when she returned with the salad, she asked, "What's YD? I understood everything else."

"YD? Yellow Dragon, of course." This was the affectionate term she used for her canary-colored Beetle that lit up the heavens when she drove it to work.

"I didn't drive it today. It's making some strange noises. I'll see you in the lobby, OK?"

"OK," I said, although I was a bit irritated that she was letting everyone at the table know that she and I would be having a top secret rendezvous in the lobby at 7:45. But no one seemed to care; they were talking about last night's baseball game.

We had finished our dessert by 6:45; two of the fellows would be going to play poker, one would watch a favorite show on TV, but not me. In the next hour I would be preparing for my "secret" meeting while Samantha was in the kitchen cleaning up.

The lobby was empty at 7:45; I sat in the corner with my notes, and a minute later Samantha breezed in. "OK, Pete, tell me everything."

"Sssssshhh. Not here, Samantha; this is too public."

She looked around and didn't see anyone.

I knew what she was going to say. "I know, Samantha, but as soon as someone comes by and sees the two of us together, they will know that we are working on another big case."

"Is it really a big case, Pete? As big as the Mafia case and the al Qaeda case?"

"Sssssssshhh." I repeated. "Maybe bigger because of the person we are working for. And it's ultra top-secret and super hush-hush, so let's go someplace where we can talk privately."

"Hmm." Samantha didn't have to think too long before coming up with a great idea. "What about Starbucks? No one would think we would be discussing top secret stuff there."

"Good idea. You drive your car and I'll drive mine."

It was crowded, and I didn't want to share a table with strangers. They might be Anglophobes or something So Samantha said, "How about Taco Bell?"

That's where we ended up and Samantha phoned her husband to tell him that she was out with a boyfriend, and she winked at me when she said that, but she told him she would be home in about a half an hour.

I was glad she put in the word *about*.

I briefed my partner in crime-fighting as quickly as I could. But briefings by an octogenarian are never brief. This time I had to tell her about my bank teller Molly even though Molly had nothing to do with our trip to London. But when I mentioned that it was Queen Elizabeth II who requested our services and that she had chosen us instead of Scotland Yard, Samantha's eyes opened as wide as I have ever seen them.

"Yes, Queen Elizabeth II," I assured her.

She was quiet for a few seconds and then asked, "Pete, you

didn't happen to know Queen Elizabeth I, did you?"

I had to excuse her. For the younger generation, anything that happened before Elvis is prehistoric, and it is difficult for them to put Tyrannosaurus Rex, Alexander the Great, and Elizabeth I on a timeline, so I smiled a fatherly smile at her and said, "The first Queen Elizabeth was just a few years before my time." Then I thought I needed to emphasize it again: "But you can't mention to anyone—and that includes your mother, your husband, your kids, or even your three dogs or do you have four now? --that we will be working for the Queen of England. Even when we come back again, we can't tell anyone the real reason for the trip. Maybe we can invent some other crime that we had been invited to solve, but we can't say that it involved Queen Elizabeth at all."

We were seated in a corner booth at Taco Bell. A few other patrons were there, but they didn't seem interested in us.

"But what's the crime that we are supposed to solve?"

"We won't know exactly what it is until we meet with the Queen. Watson IV doesn't know what it is either but he thinks it is a theft of some kind, but maybe the Queen just lost something or other. Some octogenarians do things like that, you know."

"I know, Pete, but it still sounds pretty fishy to me."

"I thought so too. But right now I have $29,000 in the bank from Watson IV who says he got it from the Queen, and I'll be writing you a check for $20,000, which you can divide between your Mom and yourself. A few thousand will go for airfare, but we will be living free of charge on the third floor of the Sherlock Holmes Museum, so our London expenses shouldn't be too bad."

"You don't know my mother in a London department store."

"But you won't tell her the real reason we are going there."

"I've told her already that it has something to do with crime-fighting, and she said that would be OK because they use billy clubs over there instead of machine guns."

Then, gradually, a broad smile evolved on her face and her eyes lit up. "When do we go?"

"Watson IV says that the Queen's personal secretary is bugging him every day to find out when we will arrive. So the ball is back in your court, Samantha. How soon can you make arrangements to leave your two jobs, your husband and kids, and your dogs, and how long will it take your Mom to get packed up? Of course, we have to get our airline tickets too."

Samantha took a last slurp of her Pepsi and slid out of our booth. "Awesome. Then let's get going. Don't just sit there, Pete. We've got a lot of work to do."

That sounded like the old Samantha.

CHAPTER 3

I had three phone calls from Watson IV in the next two days. I'm sure he was being pressured by the queen's private secretary who was being pressured by her Royal Highness.

And I had a couple phone calls from Samantha. One was about how long a trip it would be and the other about what she should wear. To the first, I said that I didn't have the foggiest idea, although we would probably become more acquainted with fogs after a few days in London, and to the second, I said, "Ask your mother." I suppose I should have been more gracious about it, because I had just completed my third conversation with Watson IV, in which I asked, "What clothes should I bring?"—which, although not the same question that Samantha had asked me (because a woman's wardrobe is different from a man's), yet it was similar in that both questions related to clothing, and the answers were different in that Watson IV didn't suggest I ask my mother, because even if she were alive she would be close to 120 by now and be surrounded by TV anchormen asking what was the secret to her longevity, and if I knew my mother, and I probably knew her as well as most people, except Aunt Lil with whom Mother was very close until Mother discovered that Aunt Lil couldn't keep a secret, and when Mother told Aunt Lil that she had fallen in love with Harry Belafonte, soon the whole community knew about it, and Mother didn't speak to Aunt Lil again ever—well, at least for two weeks when a Harry Belafonte Special was announced and Aunt Lil invited her over because Aunt Lil had just gotten a color TV set, and Mother was always ready to forgive and forget, especially the last part and to see Harry Belafonte in living color was irresistible or unforgettable, or was that Nat King Cole, the merry old soul?

I was still figuring all of that out when the phone rang again, and it was Samantha. "When are you buying the airline tickets?" She almost sounded like Watson IV—or maybe, because her voice was higher pitched, like Watson V.

Before I could answer, she continued, "I just remembered that Carmen, who volunteers with me at the Humane Society, has a friend at a travel agency who could probably get us a good deal."

"OK. Where's the travel agency? I'll meet you there in a half hour." I thought I could call her bluff. I didn't think she was ready to go yet.

"One problem. I don't have any money."

"I've got the money, honey, if you've got the time."

"Pete, what are you talking about?"

"Sorry, but that was a popular song in the 1950s."

"And that was a long time before I was born. Better not start singing it when either my husband or my mother is around."

"OK, OK. What I meant is that when I see you at the travel agency, I'll put everything on my credit card."

When I arrived at the travel agency, Samantha's Yellow Beetle was parked outside, and she was inside talking to a travel agent, who I guessed was the friend of her friend.

"Pete, this is Ariana, the one I was telling you about. I was just saying how we need a flight to London as quick and cheap as possible."

Ariana gave me a lingering handshake and looked me straight in the eyes. "I think I can make that happen, for such distinguished clients." She seemed to sparkle as she said it.

But then she turned her attention to her computer screen and tapped away at the keyboard as she tried to maintain a conversation. We learned that she was running this agency by herself, *tap tap tap*, ever since her husband had passed away two years earlier ("his final voyage"). *Tap tappety tap tap.* Business was bad and getting worse, *tap tap*, now that everybody booked their own flights on line, but *tap taptap tap* she liked putting together tour packages and cruises, so she'd keep doing that *tap tap* until she was, well, tapped out.

If she were my daughter, I would tell her she didn't need such heavy makeup and she didn't need to wear such a low-cut blouse. After all, she wasn't auditioning for a movie. She was attractive enough with her mop of jet black hair that meandered down the right side of her face to her shoulders and beyond, so that every fifteen seconds she had to flip her head to the right to get her hair back in place, although I was afraid that if she flipped her head too vigorously, the golden hoops she wore as earrings might fall off. Ariana was not a youngster, but one problem that octogenarians have is that any woman who is under sixty looks like a young woman to us. From what she was telling us about her life and work, I would guess that Ariana was in her mid-fifties, but she looked like she could be in her forties, and of course she dressed and acted like she was thirty. I don't analyze the age of every woman I meet, but something about Ariana intrigued me.

Apparently I intrigued her, too, at least in my connection with Samantha. "So, how long have you two been, uh, going together?" she asked between taps.

I was flattered and embarrassed at the same time. While I tried to figure out what to say, Samantha jumped in. "Oh, no, Ariana, you have us all wrong. Pete and I are business partners. We are not 'going together.' Well, yes, we are going together to London, and we get along well with each other, but we are not 'going together,' if you know what I mean."

Ariana smiled knowingly. "That's all right. I get that all the time: young women and older men. Usually they're going to Vegas or Cancun, not London. But whatever you say, it doesn't matter; it won't go on your ticket, you know."

Samantha was vigorously shaking her head. "Ariana, you still don't understand. My mother will be going with us. Three round-trip tickets and one is a senior, if that helps at all."

"Ah, so you two need a chaperone, is that it? It's OK, Samantha. I won't tell Carmen, even though she's my best friend. As they say in Vegas, What happens here stays here."

Just before a frustrated Samantha tried to explain again, Ariana broke into a wide grin. "I get it, I get it. I'm just teasing you. Honestly, I think it's great that the two of you can be such good friends, you know, across the generations. And I'm actually kind of glad there's no hanky-panky here, Pete. Maybe I still have a chance with you." She winked at me and flipped her head to get her hair back in place.

I was getting the idea that she worked better with male clients than with female clients. Samantha asked tersely, "So, can you get us a good flight?"

"I think this will work for you," said Ariana, back to business. "Do you need accommodations in London? I could set you up with some nice tour packages."

"No, that's taken care of. We have rooms at the—" I suddenly realized I was about to spill some beans, though I'm not sure what kind of beans I'd be spilling. Some are messier than others. "We're staying with friends." I wasn't sure if I could call Watson IV a friend yet, even though we'd been talking on the phone every day.

"How nice," the agent responded. I could tell she was curious about what I *almost* said, but maybe that would just make me more intriguing. "What about some attractions? There's a tour that would take you to Buckingham Palace. Hey, maybe you'll see the Queen."

"Maybe," I smiled. *If she only knew!* "But no, I'm sure our friends have a full schedule of activities for us while we're there."

"Great. Well, it's good to have friends."

I wasn't sure if she was upset that my British friends were taking away her business, teasing about Samantha and me being "just friends," or suggesting that she'd like to be more of a friend to me, and perhaps more than a friend. She was an assertive saleswoman; I just wasn't sure what she was selling.

Ariana tapped a few more keys and quoted me a price on the airline tickets. It was quite reasonable, I thought, so I handed her my credit card. She took it, got up slowly, glanced back at me with another smile as she smoothed down her skirt behind her, and then minced into a back room holding my card in her well-manicured hand. I was amazed at the confident way she carried herself wearing at least four inch high heels, and was still able to do it with a little swing to her hips. "She's checking me out in the back room," I told Samantha.

"I'm sure she is."

Even through the closed door, I could hear Ariana humming, though I couldn't quite name the tune. It might have been "New York, New York" or "I Left My Heart in San Francisco" or maybe "London Bridges Falling Down"—something geographical, which would only make sense for a travel agent. I bet she had a whole album of city-songs she could hum in situations like this. She had a very pleasant voice. I figured that she was making this noise to let us know that she wasn't absconding with my credit card. That was the oldest trick in the book of course, taking the card to the "back room" when you're really halfway to Albuquerque on a spending spree.

Maybe that was the song she was humming: "Halfway to Albuquerque."

At some point in the third verse, Samantha decided to wait for me in the car. Apparently she wasn't enjoying the humming as much as I was. And just when I thought this was taking far too long, Ariana reappeared with her sparkling smile and swinging hips.

"Sorry about that, Pete. I guess I'm old-fashioned, but I keep the credit card contraption in the back on an old phone line, and sometimes it's a bit cranky. But it finally went through, and everything's fine. If you just sign this, I can print out the tickets right here."

When I handed her the signed credit slip, Ariana handed me a brochure about Paris. "You might be interested in this, Pete. I'm planning to take a break in the spring and I thought maybe we could spend a week in Paris. Are you interested?"

"We?"

"*Oui, oui, monsieur!* So you *are* interested."

"Well," I back-pedaled, "it's a very interesting idea. After all, we just met."

"But there's a real chemistry between us, don't you think? A certain *je ne sais quoi.* Can't you feel it?"

"I think they served that for dinner last night. And, yes, I can still feel it."

"Forgive me if I'm being forward, but I'm tired of being lonely. And this Paris trip—well, I would love to have an experienced traveler like yourself come along with me, someone as interesting as you are. It's not that strange, really. Samantha tells Carmen about your detective work, and Carmen tells me. And here you are in my office. It's the most exciting thing that's happened to me in a long time."

I wasn't sure how to process all this. "If I'm the most exciting thing, then you have a very dull life. Sorry, that didn't sound right."

"Well, I do!" Ariana fetched the tickets from the printer and gave them to me, letting her hands linger on mine. "Look, have a great time in London, and when you get back, give me a call. Maybe we can have dinner and you can tell me all about it. And *then* we can talk more about springtime in Paris."

With that, she gave me a quick kiss on the cheek. Seeing my chance to escape, I trundled out to Samantha's car. And then I realized: that was the song Ariana had been humming. "Springtime in Paris."

CHAPTER 4

Samantha phoned early the next morning and suggested we have coffee together at the Black Bear Restaurant. She would start work at 11:00, so if I could join her at 10:30, we would have a few minutes to prepare for London.

It was all happening so fast that neither of us had more than a few minutes to do anything. All I had to do was to notify the front desk that I would be away for a couple weeks, but for Samantha with her two jobs and her volunteer work at the Humane Society, her kids, her husband, and her three dogs (or was it four), it was a much bigger effort. Besides that, as a woman, she would have to plan what she would be wearing every day, especially as a woman who would be meeting with Queen Elizabeth one day and might be down on her knees the next day searching for whatever was lost, strayed, or stolen from Buckingham Palace.

"Are you packed yet?" asked Samantha with a laugh as I approached the café table.

"Sssssssshhh," I cautioned, though the corner in which she was sitting was relatively empty.

"Sorry, I forgot," she apologized, "but I'm so excited, I can't think straight. My poor husband. He wants me to go, but he doesn't know how he can handle it all by himself, especially since

35

my mom is going with us. But I'm confident that he will manage somehow. Which is more than I can say for us."

"What do you mean?"

Samantha took a sip of coffee and kept staring down at it, shaking her head. "Seriously, I stayed up half the night thinking we should call the whole thing off. We don't know enough about the case to even consider it. I don't know a thing about London, and I don't know what or who we are looking for. Besides that, I don't have a thing to wear that would be suitable. Do you have a good suit, Pete? I've never seen you wearing a suit. If you had a wife, she would have been reminding you of such things."

"I've never even thought about that."

"Maybe you should think of re-marrying. I think Ariana might be available."

"Don't start," I warned.

"Paris in the springtime? Could be very romantic."

"I'm sorry I ever told you about that. She's just a lonely widow who . . . who . . ."

"Who thinks you are a real catch, which you are. No need to be shy about it."

"Can we forget about Ariana and Paris for now? We've got more important things to work on."

"OK," she agreed, with a roll of her eyes. "You may be sixty years older than I am, but you're still a man, and you need a woman to tell you that you need to wear a suit when you have an audience with the Queen of England." She paused to think. "At least a suit, maybe even a tux."

"For heaven's sake, Samantha, we're not going to a wedding."

"I guess not, but this might be the biggest event of your life, of our lives, and I want to be very sure we're dressed for it. You don't know how they are over there. If you don't say the proper words or wear the proper clothes, they reject you. We're going to have enough trouble convincing them that we're real detectives, without worrying about our outfits."

This was not like Samantha. She was frustrated and excited at the same time. We couldn't do any preparation because we didn't know what to prepare for, and that was frustrating. At one point, as we were finishing our coffee, she said, "You know, Pete, I would be serious about calling the whole thing off if my mom weren't so excited about going. I can't disappoint her now."

It's true. The only thing that stopped our scuttling the whole thing was Samantha's mom, although I told Samantha that I felt like Columbus when his crew wanted to mutiny. Well, I really didn't know how Columbus felt, except he was too committed to the project to turn back, and then one of his crew spotted Miami Beach in the distance and he couldn't believe how tall those high-rise condos were, so they sailed on, and another sailor said, "Si, si, and thar must be gold in them thar hills," or something like that.

That afternoon, I went to the library and took out three travel books on London, two biographies of Queen Elizabeth, and one on travel to France, the last one was only to tease Samantha and make her think that I might be serious about taking a trip to Paris, which of course I wasn't, because I wasn't thinking about Ariana at all. That may be a bit of an overstatement, but if I was thinking of her at all, it was only because Samantha kept referring to her, hinting that I might need a wife, which was absolutely ridiculous. I had a good wife, a wonderful wife for a long, long time. No one would ever replace her. So why should I think of remarrying just so I would know to wear a suit when I have an audience with the Queen.

I hoped that one of the books from the library would tell me what to wear in Buckingham Palace. A book from the Free Library was a lot cheaper than marrying a wife. Of course, I still might have to get my shirt ironed, and I doubted if the Sherlock Holmes Museum provided that service. Maybe Samantha's mom liked to iron, although then she might ask a few questions about why she shouldn't accompany us to see whoever required our detective services. Besides that, I doubted that she liked to iron. Not many people did

It was easy for me to tell the front desk in the retirement community that I would be away for two weeks. No questions were asked. They had my son's address and phone number if anything happened to me, and that was all they needed. However, at the dinner table, when I told my fellow widowers that I would be going away for two weeks, I was pelted with questions. If I would be away for a day or two, that was understandable, but for two weeks? And I couldn't give them any hints, because that would only prompt more questions. It must mean that I or a close relative of mine were dying. One fellow suggested that maybe I was trying out another retirement community.

"Will you tell us all about it when you come back?"

"Oh, sure."

"If you're going to Hawaii, bring us each a coconut."

"No, I'm not going to Hawaii." I felt I was playing Twenty Questions.

"Overseas?"

"I'm not answering any more questions."

"London, Rome, or Paris?"

"I said I wasn't going to answer any more questions."

"Yeah, but I can tell we're getting close; you twitched a little when I said Paris."

Somebody else had a brainstorm. "I bet you're going to solve a case." Then a pause. "Is Samantha going with you?"

"I think the server is waiting for us to order."

And just then Samantha walked to our table, which got the questions going again. I tried to communicate with Samantha by shaking my head woefully and then putting it down on my chest.

After giving his order, one of the fellows asked Samantha, "Are you going with Pete?"

"Oh, is Pete going somewhere?" Samantha played it well. She wasn't going to give them a clue.

"Well, he's not saying much, but when we suggested Rome, London or Paris, we thought we caught a spark."

"Oh, you caught a spark, did you? I don't know because he doesn't confide in me regarding his personal matters. But if there was a spark, my guess is that it might have been when you mentioned Paris. I better not say more. Now, let's finish with your orders. Pete, you're next. Soup and salad as usual, right? And with French dressing." Of course, she hung onto the word *French*. She was enjoying this too much.

When the food came, the men stopped the guessing game, and I was thankful. I said that I would tell them all about it when I came back, "but I can't say any more now." Then I added, "But I can tell you this much: In spite of what Samantha was hinting, I am not planning to visit Paris in the next two weeks."

I thought that would be enough to halt any rumors in their tracks.

Returning to my room, I opened my suitcase on the bed and started tossing things into it—socks, underwear, T-shirts, one handkerchief. Except when we had an audience with the queen, I wanted to dress like the typical American octogenarian tourist, although I realized that most typical American tourists are not octogenarians and that made it difficult to plan. I was never good at stuffing things in suitcases; things tended to get wrinkled. My wife had been good at it, and I still missed her a lot, but whenever it came to either suitcase-packing or gift-wrapping, I missed her much more than a lot. But then the phone rang, and it was Samantha, of course.

The flight left the next morning.

On the plane everyone was civil and civilized. Samantha's mom had the window seat, and I had the aisle with Samantha in the middle. I took the aisle seat because I had seen the ocean before.

Besides that, Samantha and I had to plan our strategy for solving the mystery, whatever and wherever it was, and I needed to instruct Samantha in how to speak English as the natives do. Tourists are allowed to get away with improper speech, but if we were working for the Queen we might be held to a higher standard. And since I had been to England twice in my eighty-plus years and had spent a total of six or seven days touring the island, it was my obligation to acquaint Samantha with the facts of British speech.

So my lesson began this way: "Who's that lady next to you, Samantha?"

"My mother."

"No, it's not. She's your mum."

"My mum?"

"Yes, and as long as we are in England, you will call her 'Mum.'"

"OK, Pete, Mum's the word."

"Good. Now in London, we will be staying at the Sherlock Holmes museum, and where did I tell you that your room would be?"

"I think you said that my mother and I—I mean Mum and I—would be on the third floor."

"I meant the second floor."

"Oh good, then we can walk up. We won't need to use the elevator."

"England doesn't have any elevators."

"But they have a lot of tall buildings."

"They use lifts instead."

"I sometimes put lifts in my shoes, but I know I couldn't use them to get up to the second floor."

Then I apologized to her. After all, if she could have some fun teasing me about Ariana, I could have some fun teasing her about the English language. In England, I told her, what we call the first floor they call the ground floor, and our second floor is what they call the first floor. A lift is their name for an elevator. And at that point I stood up slowly, which is the only way I know to stand up these days, and said, "I have to go to the loo."

"The what?" she asked, a little too loud for my comfort.

"The loo," I answered more calmly. "I'll explain when I get back."

When I returned to my seat, she smiled and said, "You don't have to explain. Mum told me about the loo."

Shades were being drawn in the plane and a movie was starting. Samantha's "mum" was trying to get some sleep and was resting her head against the window. I thought Samantha would be plugging in her earpiece and watching the movie. But five seconds after she got herself plugged in, she unhooked herself, turned to me and said, "Pete, I'm scared; aren't you?"

"Me? Scared? Why should I be? Queen Elizabeth is a human being just as we are."

"Oh, I don't mean her, although that's one aspect of it. I mean the whole thing."

"The whole ball of wax, huh?" But I'd never held a ball of wax in my hand and I didn't think Samantha had a ball of wax in her purse. Maybe her mum did, but I doubted it. I decided to ask Watson IV about balls of wax. He went to Oxford. That might be the kind of thing that they learn there. I can imagine a few Oxford dons got Ph. D.'s for writing their theses on the subject.

"Pete, you're not listening. I was asking you a question about whether you are a little bit frightened by all of this. Be serious."

I was serious, but sometimes being serious and being honest are two different things. If you have a young child who is afraid of thunder, you try to convince that child not to be scared, even though lightning may have struck your family's home when you were young, and you still haven't gotten over it. I knew Samantha was not a little girl, but she was depending on me as the seasoned detective to be fearless in the face of insurmountable odds, and I had to keep up a good front, and maybe a good back as well.

So I answered, "Listen, we have faced al Qaeda and the Mafia; why should you be afraid of going to England and solving a little problem for the Queen?"

"Pete, you didn't answer my question. I was asking whether you were afraid, and you didn't answer, so I think I know that you're just as frightened as I am."

The best way to cope with fear is to take it out of its cage and see what it really is. So I told her, "Try to analyze your fear." I sounded like one of those shrinks on TV.

She paused for ten seconds and came up with her answer. Samantha thinks more quickly than I do. "OK, Pete, I think I am afraid right now, because I am afraid of failing."

"I don't think you ever failed at anything."

"Ha! That's a laugh. Don't ask my 'mum' because she could probably take the rest of the plane ride to tell you, but she wouldn't, because she wouldn't want to hurt my feelings. But what I mean, Pete, is that you've written up a couple stories and they somehow got into Buckingham Palace and now the Queen believes everything you wrote, and she thinks it's all true, and that we can solve all of her problems and probably all of the world's problems."

"Are you implying that Pete and Samantha are fakes?"

"Well, aren't we?"

It took me fifteen seconds, maybe twenty, to come up with an answer. "No, Samantha, no, we're not; at least not totally, not completely. We've never taken any money from anyone fraudulently, have we?" That big word just came to my mind as I was talking.

"No, Pete, we haven't. In fact, we have never gotten a red cent from any case we have solved, and my husband was wondering why not."

"A red cent? You're right, and not a silver or gold cent either. And they are worth more than red cents."

"But then your friend Watson the Fifth sent us the Queen's money to fly to England, so now we can be accused of taking money—*royal* money—over false pretenses."

"First of all, it's not Watson the Fifth; it's Watson the Fourth. Not *over* false pretenses, but maybe *under* false pretenses. By the way, Samantha, what was your major in college?'

"Yeah, it was Criminal Justice, and I specialized in crime scene investigation, but I've been serving tables in retirement communities ever since, and I know that you had six weeks of basic training as a military policeman sixty years ago, but now we are asked to solve something that Scotland Yard can't even solve, *and we don't even know what it is!*'

"By the way, when you're in London, don't refer to my experience as an M.P. In America that may be a military policeman but in England an M.P is a member of Parliament."

"But, Pete, you don't sound as if any of this frightens you."

"Who said that? It's just that both of us can't afford to be frightened at the same time."

"OK, then, let's take turns. But you'll have to tell me when it's your turn."

"Listen, Samantha, I don't know you as well as your mum does, but I think that as soon as we have our first meeting with Queen Elizabeth, you will be treating her just as you treat the women at the retirement home, and she will be loving it."

"I'm not sure about the Queen liking me, but I think her dogs will. I can have her dogs eating out of my hand within a half hour."

"Now, that's where we're different. Dogs frighten me; queens don't."

CHAPTER 5

I didn't know they made nights this long any more. I decided to write my congressman about it. If they could pass a Daylight Savings Law giving us more hours in the day, why couldn't they pass a Night-time Losing Law giving us fewer hours of darkness?

I couldn't blame the airlines. They seemed to be working on something. But I thought their primary aim was to keep you from sleeping. They provided a meal, plus drinks, two feature films and two stewardesses who asked, "Everything OK?" every half hour. In fact, every time I was getting settled down, something happened to wake me up. If it wasn't a movie, it was Samantha. Whenever a new movie was being introduced, she would jab me in the ribs and ask, "Have you seen this one yet?" or else Samantha would let me know that her mum was still sleeping. I was glad somebody was.

And once, when she jabbed me, she whispered, "I bet you were dreaming that Ariana was sitting next to you."

"I thought you weren't going to talk about Ariana."

"I wouldn't talk about her if you wouldn't dream about her."

"Oh, stop it, Samantha, How do you know what I was dreaming about? Now stop talking and let me sleep."

"I think you are enjoying your dream so much that you don't want me to disturb it. So go ahead and dream, while I worry about important matters like the Queen's problems."

"I wasn't dreaming and I certainly wasn't sleeping either." I knew she was teasing me, but I didn't want to be teased at four in the morning or whatever unearthly hour it was.

I hoped that Watson IV didn't have any appointments scheduled for us before I had a nap. Maybe I had forgotten to tell him that octogenarians require naps, sometimes even two a day. I wondered if Queen Elizabeth took naps. I wondered also if anyone in history had ever fallen asleep while having an audience with the queen.

I thought I had finally fallen asleep when I was jabbed in the ribs again and heard a voice saying, "I see some light out the window. Is it morning already? It sure was a short night."

I grumbled something, and the voice asked, "I'm sorry; I guess I woke you up." Maybe it would have been better if Samantha's mum had been in the middle seat.

Of course, as soon as passengers saw light out the window, the lines to the "loo" began to form, and even those who weren't in a hurry to make a morning nature call were standing in the aisle to make sure their legs were still working. I stood in the aisle for both reasons.

Soon the announcement came that we would be landing at Terminal 5, and that concerned me because the last time I was in London, I was sure that Heathrow didn't have five terminals.

"When was the last time you saw London," asked Samantha, who was standing behind me in line.

I tried to think. "It wasn't so long ago."

"In this century or the last?"

"Well, it had to have been the last, because I haven't gone across the pond in the last twenty years."

"Before the 1990s?"

"Yeah, I guess it was."

"Then it was before I was born and that was a long, long time ago."

"Maybe to you, but not to me." That ended the conversation.

Another announcement came. "All passengers must return to their seats. We will be experiencing some turbulence for the next thirty minutes, so for your safety, please return to your seats."

We returned to our seats and buckled up again for an uncomfortable thirty minutes before we were free to move around the cabin again. The attendants came around with wet washcloths to help us wake up, and eventually we were on the ground.

Now Samantha's mother was leaning over and they were both asking me questions that I couldn't answer . . . like what Watson IV looked like. I said most of the Englishmen I knew were rather tall and gaunt. No, Samantha's mum said, she knew an Englishman once who was short and had a big pot belly. But Samantha said that the English all love to play soccer, and so they must be in pretty good shape. And I wondered how they can keep in shape, if it is raining most of the time. And then Samantha said something about riding horses in the steeplechase or watching dogs chase foxes, and I knew that I had to put up with that kind of talk because Samantha was interested in horses and dogs, and I said the sport that I am more interested in is curling and you can play it when it's raining outside and when you have a big pot belly. And Samantha said that she hoped there was a pub near where we were staying, and her mum said, "I hope you don't plan on spending all your time in pubs."

Before we knew it, we were getting off the plane and Samantha was phoning her husband to tell him that the plane hadn't fallen into the Atlantic or anything, and that I had behaved myself well because her "mum" was along. Her husband must have asked who that was, because Samantha had to explain that "Britishers talk about their mothers that way."

With an international flight, I don't know if there's more hassle in getting on or getting off. They asked if we had anything to declare, and I didn't remember what that meant. I was sure they weren't still miffed about our Declaration of Independence, but just in case, I told Samantha and her mother to declare nothing. That seemed to help. I was afraid they might ask us to recite the entire Declaration in unison; I seemed to remember the first three words as "We the people," but maybe that was Lincoln's Gettysburg Address.

We stood in line—no, not a line but a queue—which is another thing I needed to tell Samantha. London doesn't have lines; it has queues. They may look like lines, but they aren't, because Brits are more polite than Americans, and no one breaks into a queue. They may not be able to spell it, but they can't break into it.

And then, Shirley, Samantha's mom, burst out with, "I see him. Look, Samantha. That must be him over there. He's holding a sign, and he looks just like Winston Churchill. I'd know him anywhere."

Finally, Samantha noticed the man her mum was pointing to. "No, he doesn't look like Churchill; he looks more like Ringo Starr."

I didn't know what they were talking about, but the sign said, "Welcome to London, Dr. Petersen," and I remembered him telling me during the last phone call that he would have a welcoming sign in the arrival area that only I would recognize. "In England," he had said, "we don't call a person by his first name unless we know him extremely well, and we hardly ever use a first name for a woman unless it's a family member."

"Doesn't he look like Ringo Starr?" Samantha asked me when the queue got to the gate.

Sometimes one has to be diplomatic in cases like that. "Well, I think he looks like a cross between Churchill and Ringo Starr." I don't know if that pleased either the mother or the daughter. I couldn't imagine what a Churchill-Starr cross would look like, but I knew such a person would certainly be star-crossed. When I finally met him, I didn't know how to address him. Was he Dr. Watson IV or "Blimey, if it isn't my old matey, Johnny"? I finally settled on "Dr. Watson, I presume."

He said he had no trouble picking us out of the crowd: he just looked for "an attractive young woman, an attractive mother, and an equally attractive octogenarian in his own way." As an Oxford graduate, he was obviously careful in picking his words, but I didn't know why he needed to add "in his own way."

He told the two women to wait inside while he and I walked out and waited for his driver to pull the car around, "He has probably been circling the oval for a half hour," Watson said.

"Is the plane late?" I asked. I didn't know the time. My watch wouldn't have been any help. I couldn't remember if London was eight or nine hours ahead of us or eight or nine behind.

"No, only a half hour late, and the airlines regard that as on time." Watson looked at his watch and added, "Roger should be here in another minute or two."

"Your chauffeur?"

"Oh, no, Roger is a student at the University here and comes over to visit with me at the Museum to be tutored in Eighteenth

Century British Literature. But we put him to work. He dresses the part of Sherlock and, of course, I play Watson. The tutoring usually gets done after hours. But when he is my chauffeur he wears a chauffeur's cap. It will help us today at Buckingham. Royalty is impressed with uniforms."

"Buckingham today?" I asked.

Just then he spotted Roger and waved him to a stop. Roger stopped directly in front of us and proceeded to get off on the wrong side of the car. Then I saw that the steering wheel was on the wrong side of the car too. "Don't they know how to make cars here?" I wondered, before I recalled that in England they also made their roads backwards. The roads must have come first, and since they had already put up their signs on the wrong side of the road, they had to design automobiles accordingly. So now I remembered: You drive on the left side of the road and their steering wheels are on the right side of the car, but most of the world drives on the right side of the road with steering wheels on the left. Go figure!

While I was pondering, Watson IV, alias Winston-Ringo, was telling the non-chauffeur Roger to go inside and bring out the two American ladies and their bags, or something like that. But he ended his instruction, "Don't hurry, because we have some things to discuss privately."

As soon as Roger left, I repeated my question, "Buckingham today?"

"Yes. Sorry about that, ol' chap. You see, first thing this morning I had a phone call from the queen's personal secretary, telling me that there was an opening on the queen's docket at 2:30 this afternoon and that it was imperative that you and Samantha be there. And I asked, 'What if the airplane arrives late?' And she answered, 'It had better not be late because the airline depends on government subsidies, and this is a matter of the highest priority to the queen.' The secretary, who usually knows everything, doesn't seem to know any more about this case than I know, and I have told you everything I know."

I nodded.

He motioned with his head in the direction of the two women, "But her mum doesn't even know that much?" He said it as a question, but he hoped it was a fact.

"All her mum knows," I assured him, "is that we have been asked to come here by some government officials."

"I guess you can call the queen a government official," Watson IV commented, and I thought he almost smiled when he said it. Then, very seriously, he asked, "How long does it take Samantha to change clothes?"

I was going to say, "How should I know?" But instead after a few seconds, I said, "All I know is that Samantha is quick in everything she does, so my guess is that she can get dressed faster than the average woman." I had no idea how long it took an average woman to change clothes, but I knew that Samantha would be faster than that.

I had to inform Watson, "Honestly, sir, I was hoping for a little nap before I visited the queen."

"When you are working for the queen you do not have time for naps."

"But I'm an octogenarian."

"Yes, I know. You are the octogenarian sleuth. It is written in capital letters on all your books. But Queen Elizabeth is four years older than you are, and her secretary tells me that naps aren't on her calendar."

I could see that Watson didn't care for excuses.

Emerging from the terminal came Roger followed by a cart with the luggage and the two women tagging along behind. Watson asked me, "What did you say was the name of Samantha's mum?"

"Shirley," I answered quickly. "But I didn't think you usually called women by their first names here."

"We make exceptions. And by the way, you won't have to worry about Shirley's well-being in London. I will be happy to be her escort."

"But who will handle the visitors at the museum?"

"Roger will be able to substitute for me. He looks a lot like Sherlock, you know."

On the way to the Sherlock Holmes Museum on Baker Street, I sat in the front with Roger, while Watson IV crunched into the back with the women. The noisy traffic and the roundabouts, plus my hearing problems, made it difficult for me to hear what they were talking about in the back seat, but I assumed that Watson IV was explaining the afternoon's schedule to them.

At one point I heard Samantha raise her voice. "You've got to be kidding. Pete, tell me that Mr. Watson is just kidding."

I turned my head to say, "I couldn't hear what he said, but I don't think that Mr. Watson kids very often."

"But twenty minutes to get ready for an audience with the que. . ." and she caught herself in time to finish the sentence with "I mean the quoit cotillion." I didn't know what a quoit cotillion was, and I doubted that Samantha did either, but it sounded very British.

Shirley helped out by saying, "Cotillions are a lot of fun, Samantha. You'll enjoy it."

Watson added, "You'll look hunky-dory no matter what you wear."

To that comment Samantha simply wrinkled her nose. I would have done the same, but I never learned how to wrinkle my nose.

Watson also made some other comments that didn't matter to us--like saying that the museum isn't really at 221B Baker Street, as it says in the books, but it's between 237 and 241 Baker Street, which we didn't care about, although if we were giving directions to a cab driver, it might be useful. "But we have a sign that says 221B Baker on the front of the building anyway," Watson said.

When we got there, Samantha climbed out of the car first and galloped up the stairs with a full head of steam. The rest of us waited for the lift.

"When she starts moving," said Shirley, "you'd better get out of her way."

I looked at my watch and then to Watson, "Twenty minutes?"

"Actually, twenty-five, but when you are meeting the queen, it is preferable to be five minutes early than five minutes late."

One thing I realized in those twenty minutes was that octogenarians do not get dressed as quickly as young people do. By the time I got to the sitting room, Samantha was already there, all smiles, and asking, "What took you so long?"

She looked like a female CEO dressed for a conference with her board of directors. "You look great." I said.

"Mom bought it for me two days ago. It's really nothing special." The outfit was a simple black and white affair--a black jacket with a knee-length polka-dotted dress and a large white belt.

"I say it's perfect," offered Watson. "You know, the queen isn't impressed with women who go to extravagant lengths and display the latest fashions. But you look chic and smart. Her Majesty will be impressed."

"But," I intruded, half in jest, "I'm going to see the queen too, and no one has remarked about my outfit."

"You're fine," Samantha said. "I've never seen you in a suit-coat before."

On the way to Buckingham Palace, Watson gave us some background. It has been the residence of British royalty since 1761, when King George III bought the palace from the Duke of Buckingham. But Brits as well as tourists from other countries never saw the inside of the place until Queen Elizabeth opened up part of it to the public. Entrance fees helped to pay for the restoration of another royal residence, Windsor Castle, which had been damaged by fire in 1992. Now in the peak months of tourism, 7,000 visitors a day walk through Buckingham. Of course, the residences of the Queen and the Duke of Edinburgh on the north side of the palace are private and so are the upper-floor apartments where other members of the royal family live.

Samantha interrupted. "I don't care about the royal apartments. I want to see where they keep the horses."

The horses, Watson explained, are kept in the Royal Mews, which is open even when Buckingham is closed.

"Mews? It sounds like it's the place where the royal cats are kept."

"Yes, it's a strange word. Actually, it comes from the sound of sea gulls. The royal hawks are also caged there, and so you can hear lots of mewing in the royal mews. The Royal Mews are quite interesting for other reasons too. The royal coaches and cars as well as horses are kept there."

"Pete, let's plan on going there some day after our other work, whatever it is, is completed. And 'Mum' would like to visit the Royal Mews too."

I was looking to see how much of London I could recognize from my last visit thirty years ago, but Roger didn't give me any time to ask questions. I recognized Hyde Park with its famous

Speakers Corner, and, of course, when we got to Piccadilly, I remembered the name.

"Pete, you're probably remembering Piccadilly Circus. That's the circle or roundabout that opens up to the main shopping area to one side and the theatre district to the other." Watson IV was now calling me Pete; but to me he wasn't John yet.

"And now, we're at the Palace." I'm sure it was just as awesome to Samantha as it was to me, maybe more so.

We stopped at the gate. A guard came to check us out. From the back seat, Watson called out, "We have an appointment with the queen in less than a half hour."

"By whose permission."

"By the permission of Edward Young, deputy private secretary to the queen."

"The vehicle can proceed to the next gate, and then it must turn around and go back out. Two people will be allowed to get out of the vehicle and they can proceed on foot to the next kiosk."

The guard had his lines well memorized. Roger drove slowly about fifty yards to a second gate. Watson then instructed Samantha and me what to do next. This guard had a list of names which should include ours. We got out of the car, and Watson reminded us, in case we were stopped again, to remember the name of Edward Young and to say that the queen had requested our services.

We watched Roger and Watson go back through the first gate. After we took about ten steps toward the palace, Samantha stopped and pulled against my suitcoat. She pointed to the huge building. "Pete, we're going in there?"

I took another look at the palace. From this perspective it looked even larger than it looked from Buckingham Gate.

"Yeah, Samantha, I guess that's what we agreed to do."

"I can't do it."

"Yes, you can, Samantha. We've solved every case we have been given, haven't we?"

"But those weren't real cases, Pete. They were all in your imagination. But this is a real palace, and Queen Elizabeth thinks we are real detectives who can solve her problem whatever it is. But we're frauds, and you know it."

"You're wrong. You're a real person and I'm a real person and . . ."

"And what, Pete, what are we going to do?

"We're going to try, Samantha. The two of us are going to try."

I remembered what I said to her on the plane that only one of us could afford to be afraid at any one time. So I couldn't afford to tell her how I really felt. Instead, I put my arm behind her back and started her moving again.

We passed two small kiosks at which we gave our names. They checked their list, which fortunately (or unfortunately, depending how you look at it) included our names. The closer we got to the palace, the more enormous it became. I was awestruck too, but I shrugged my shoulders to indicate "if you've seen one palace you've seen them all." After all, I think I remember going to Versailles fifty years ago, or was it the Louvre?

As we stood in the entrance, Samantha seemed paralyzed. I nudged Samantha inside, where a young woman was waiting, who called us by name. I could tell that Samantha relaxed a little when her name was announced. Then the woman introduced herself as the private secretary to the queen's deputy private secretary. (I didn't know if all of that would fit on a normal business card, but maybe she didn't need a business card.). Then she took us down a long hall to what she called an antechamber and what I called a waiting room. I looked at my watch. We had three minutes to spare.

"Pete, pinch me. I don't think this is real."

CHAPTER 6

Waiting rooms are boring, no matter what you call them. You can dress them up by calling them antechambers, reception lounges or audience salons, but they are still boring.

Even the thumbed-over magazines they have are boring. The paintings on the wall are boring. The walls themselves, done in a pale eggshell hue, are super-boring. It would have added a little excitement if someone had thrown actual eggs at the walls. Then they could have labeled each eggshell with the thrower's name: "Flung by Winston Churchill, March 5, 1942;" "Tossed underhand by Margaret Thatcher, October 7, 1985;" "Lobbed by Neville Chamberlain, September 21, 1939."

The private secretary to the deputy private secretary returned to tell us that it wouldn't be long. I've heard the same line used in countless restaurants and doctor's offices in America. "Long" is always longer when you don't know exactly what awaits you on the other side of the door. In the waiting room of a dentist's office, *it won't be long* may feel like an endless torment.

"Who's in there now?" I asked. Conversation can make the time far faster.

"Can't say."

"Somebody important?" I asked.

"Can't say."

Now Samantha entered the conversation: "Don't badger her, Pete. You know that audiences with the queen are kept confidential."

The private secretary nodded in agreement with Samantha's comment, but I wasn't satisfied. "I think she knows more than she's telling. After all, she's the private secretary to the deputy private secretary to the queen. I bet she also knows why we are seeing the queen."

"Pete, NO," and then Samantha glared at me in the same way my mother used to glare at me more than seventy years ago. She didn't have to say more; I felt chastised. Samantha might be sixty years my junior, but she had a powerful glare that I hadn't seen too often.

When I quieted down, Samantha spoke quietly to the private secretary. I didn't hear the first part of the conversation, but I know that Samantha discovered the secretary's name and told her that we might be returning again in the next two weeks. I think we were the "good cop, bad cop" routine to perfection.

Although I was admittedly a bit miffed when Samantha put me in my place, I was pleased that Samantha was stepping out of her cocoon. A few minutes earlier, she was paralyzed with fear, but she was coping now. And Samantha had always been a good coper. Maybe it was now my turn to admit I was scared stiff.

"Dragon Lady," or whatever her name was, asked Samantha if we had ever been to Buckingham Palace before, and Samantha said, "I haven't, but I don't know about. . ."

The secretary apparently didn't care if I had seen the palace before, so she launched into her spiel before Samantha finished her sentence. She said something about the palace having nearly 800 rooms, including almost 200 staff bedrooms and about 80 bathrooms. She didn't call them loos. Even British octogenarians must be sure a bathroom is not far away. She also said there were 19 state rooms where the queen meets special guests, and "you will be meeting the queen in the state room called the White Drawing Room." The Dragon Lady looked at me, almost rolling her eyes and wondering how we qualified as "special guests," but she was trained not to ask questions.

A little green light started blinking. Samantha's new friend noticed it, smiled at Samantha (not at me) and said, "You and your grandfather may go in now."

I was about to correct her. Samantha, guessing that I might be opening my mouth, put her index finger over her lips as if to say "Sssssssshhh," or maybe "Shut your trap."

Then the secretary opened the door to the White Drawing Room and introduced us. "Your Majesty, may I present," but I wasn't listening. Maybe I had been dumbed down by the drabness of the antechamber, but the White Drawing room was magnificent. It looked thirty feet high; everything was in brilliant yellow, not white, but the yellow was a golden yellow. Samantha's car, her Yellow Dragon, would have fit in well with the décor.

And then I noticed the queen—how could I not notice?—she was dressed in white, the only white in the white drawing room.

And then out of the corner of my eye, I noticed that Samantha was doing a cute little curtsy, and I remembered that I was supposed to do something too, so I took one step forward, led with my head, and began to stumble. I took two more short steps forward to stabilize myself and I felt Samantha's hand reaching out to keep me from falling farther. I don't know if it qualified as a bow or not, but if I had gone farther I would be lying flat on my face in front of royalty. And that would certainly have qualified as a bow.

I straightened up, looked at the queen, and noticed a slight smile on her face. In my almost-falling move, I might have lost a button from my suit coat, but I wasn't going to get down on the floor and search for it. Maybe later. Now we had more important things to do.

I heard Queen Elizabeth saying, "I've read about you in your books, but now I want to know about you in real life. Samantha, tell me about yourself."

"Well, I . . ." She cleared her throat.

Samantha is usually very quick with a reply, so I thought she needed some help this time, and I interrupted to say, "She has one husband, two jobs, three children and four dogs, besides working at an animal shelter." I thought the summary would be appreciated. Samantha would probably take five minutes to say the same thing.

The queen glared at me. There was that glare again. I hate glares. But along with the glare, the Queen said in no uncertain terms, "Interruptions are not permitted during an audience with the queen, so I will ask you to be quiet while I talk some more with Samantha."

I decided to be quiet. Twice within the past five minutes I had been put in my place by a woman. So I let the two of them carry on their conversation without my help even though, more than once, I could have clarified matters for them. The queen, of course, was most interested in Samantha's love of dogs. And soon they were talking about the queen's favorite breeds. Samantha was very interested in the whole subject, but I couldn't care less that King George V, Elizabeth's grandfather, bred Labradors, nor that the queen had continued his breeding program. It was her father, she said, who introduced her to corgis, and gave her one as a present on her eighteenth birthday. She now had five corgis and two dorgis, which are apparently a cross between a corgi and a dachshund.

It was a lot of dog talk and I was afraid that the queen would never get around to telling us the real reason she had asked us to come to London. I almost interrupted again to suggest that we get down to business, but I thought that if I did, I might be banished to the Tower of London for life, or else to a gaol on a remote island in the North Sea.

Finally she said, "Now, both of you must listen closely because this is of utmost importance not only to me and also to the Commonwealth of the fifty-four countries that I lead."

I perked up.

"I do not know how to impress upon you the magnitude of your mission or the secrecy in which you must conduct it. Perhaps I could liken it to 9/11 in your country. It is similar to that in its magnitude."

I was listening with both ears. My hearing aid was listening too, and that was important.

Then, for the first time, she addressed me, "Do you understand?"

"Yes, your Majesty."

"And both of you are certain that your mission has not been compromised."

It was one of those "difficult to answer" questions. Did a *No* mean that we weren't certain or did it mean "No, our mission has not been compromised"? I started to say no, but when I realized that Samantha was saying yes, I changed my vote to "Nyes." Anyway, the Queen seemed satisfied.

"And neither your husband, your mother, nor your children know anything about it?" The queen looked at Samantha first and she replied quickly, "No, your majesty; only that we are working on a special case in England."

Then the queen looked at me. "And neither your children nor your lady friends know anything about it." I didn't dare look at Samantha but I was sure she was enjoying the reference to lady friends. "No, they don't, your Majesty," I answered. That was a clear response for the queen, but I didn't know if that would mean to Samantha that I had a lady friend. I would have to clarify that answer later to Samantha.

The queen must have pushed a button somewhere, because the door suddenly opened. The queen summoned the secretary with a sharp "Clarice," pronouncing the last syllable as 'ice"— which I thought was appropriate. "Would you retrieve my itinerary for the last two weeks of last month?"

When the private secretary to the deputy private secretary left, the queen said, "And no one in the Royal Family, with the exception of my husband, Prince Philip, knows anything about it either. And it is difficult to keep anything a secret in this family." She almost smiled, which would be an unqueenly thing to do.

"Here is the story: About two months ago, the Sultan of Oman, a rather small but important nation on the Arabian Gulf, had an audience with me, and presented me with a gift from Oman, and this is common on the part of visiting dignitaries."

I nodded to indicate that I had heard of Oman. I had also heard of Yemen, and I thought there should also be an emirate of "No ma'am" to even things out.

"His gift was a very lovely brooch inscribed with some Arabic letters on it, and I wore it for the remainder of the month to show my appreciation to the nation of Oman."

We both nodded. When you are with a queen, it is better to move your head vertically than horizontally.

She continued, "For the next two weeks, I wore it to various festivities. It was a very attractive brooch, and on its reverse side were two inscriptions, one in English and a longer one in Arabic. The English inscription was very complimentary and I assumed the Arabic inscription, which was longer, was even more complimentary. I asked Prince Philip if he could read the Arabic inscription because he has spent more time in that part of the world than I have. He made out a few words, but he wasn't sure of the rest. So he made an etching of it and sent it to an Arabic scholar at the British Museum, while I continued to wear it to various functions.

"Then one afternoon when I returned to the royal apartments, I noticed that I no longer was wearing the brooch, and I told that to Prince Philip. He responded that it was just as well that it was lost or stolen, because the Arabic inscription said, 'Elizabeth II, monarch of the Commonwealth, is a secret believer in Allah, and will soon renounce her Christianity and convert to Islam.'

"Prince Philip laughed at it and called it silliness, but it was very serious to me. Can you imagine if the tabloids published this around the world? Worse yet, I have been wearing this brooch and photographs of me wearing the brooch have been published in Arab lands.

"You see, my official title is 'head of the Commonwealth and Defender of the Faith.' I am the leader of the worldwide Anglican Church with eighty-five million members, and I take my Christian faith seriously. I am a Christian, a devoted Christian."

Both Samantha and I continued to nod at appropriate times. When the Queen paused a few seconds, I took a chance to say something without jeopardizing my well-being.

"Might the brooch have been stolen?" I asked.

"Prince Philip suggested that, too. And it was a possibility. But if it were stolen by an ordinary thief, he would fence it or hold it for ransom, so to speak. In either case, we would know about it. And if it were taken by a Muslim who knew of the inscription, it wouldn't be kept secret. So it seems logical that one of the clasps on the back of the brooch was not secure enough to hold it to my dress and it fell to the ground or to the floor."

The atmosphere had changed now. Queen Elizabeth seemed to welcome our input. Both Samantha and I were asking questions, and the Queen was very open in her answers.

She and Prince Philip had made certain that the brooch wasn't on the grounds of Buckingham Palace, but during the last two weeks of last month she had made five royal visits. "I am not traveling as much as I used to," she said, and looking at me, added, "You understand."

I understood. In fact, I understood as only another octogenarian could understand that at a certain point naps become more important than trips. In fact, I was hoping this audience with the Queen would end soon so I could operate under covers for a few hours.

The Queen pushed her little buzzer again to summon Clarice. "She should have the printout of my itinerary by now."

Clarice entered, bowed gracefully, and said, "I believe this is what you requested, your Majesty."

The Queen took the papers, looked at them briefly, and said, "This is exactly what I wanted. Thank you, Clarice."

After Clarice left, Queen Elizabeth gave the itinerary printout to Samantha. "I don't need to see it; I have memorized the five places, and I have thought about them, and I am quite sure that in the hustle and bustle associated with one of those five places, the brooch was dislodged and fell off. You two must find it."

"We are honored, Your Majesty," Samantha said, clutching the itinerary, "but in spite of Pete's novels," she nodded toward me, "we are really amateurs. Why did you not call upon Scotland Yard? You have experts, just as good as our FBI, and they know all these five places very well."

"No doubt you are right, my dear, but secrecy is my first concern. If one of the fine detectives of the Yard finds the brooch, he will no doubt keep the words of the inscription secret for a year and maybe five years, but when he retires, he will tell all to one of the tabloids, and it will be published as gospel truth.

"I know that you two are amateurs, and that is why I have summoned you from America. Even if you disclose it in one of your future novels, no one will believe you anyway. The whole story is too preposterous. Why would Queen Elizabeth ask two novices to undertake such an important mission? It doesn't make sense, does it?"

We were nodding again.

And I thought I detected a rare smile on the Queen's face.

"Thank you," she said. "You may leave, but of course, I expect to receive a progress report from you in the next few days. You may notify Clarice what places you have visited, and if you need additional information from me, you may ask Clarice to see if she can schedule another audience."

"Thank you, Your Majesty," we both said in unison.

Somewhere I had read that you were supposed to back up when leaving the Queen, so I started to leave in that manner, but I tripped again, and Samantha's arm kept me from further embarrassing myself. I heard the Queen's high-pitched voice say, "You may turn around. It is more important for a detective to know where he is going than it is to see where he has been."

When we finally stepped out of Buckingham Palace, I turned to Samantha and said, "Wow!"

And she said, "Wow."

I said, "Unbelievable."

And she said, "Awesome."

CHAPTER 7

S omething woke me up. I don't know if it was the unearthly odor that had wafted its way up to the first floor bedroom or if it was Samantha's voice yelling "Rain?"

I didn't like the smell of the first nor the sound of the second.

I turned to ask my roommate Watson IV what was going on, but he wasn't there. His bed was empty. Not only was it empty, but it was made. I hate people who make their bed before breakfast. I could go a week without making mine.

My watch told me it was five after, but I didn't know what it was five after. I should have set my watch to London time when I arrived yesterday. The clock on Watson IV's dresser told me the time in Roman numerals. I'm sure that would have helped Julius Caesar, but it took me two precious minutes to figure it out even though I had taken high school Latin. It was now seven after eight.

I started figuring out other things too, like what was the smell ascending from the ground floor. I knew that the Brits used to enjoy fried kippers for breakfast, but the younger generation didn't enjoy the smell any more than I did. I don't know what they chose instead—maybe Froot Loops, Count Chocula, or Cocoa Puffs. But I figured out that in a place like this which celebrated Sherlock Holmes, Watson IV had to start the day with smoked herring or kippers, because that was what Sherlock Holmes loved, even though it might take a week to get the taste out of your system.

I also figured out that Samantha might be waiting for me to come downstairs to make our plans for the day. Knowing Samantha, I think she already made them.

Octogenarians often need more pre-breakfast time because our minds are so busy figuring out vital things like that.

I also wondered if it would be OK if I asked for a side order of Wheaties to go with the kippers. I hoped they had a dog which I could feed under the table. I'm sure a British dog would love kippers.

Arriving downstairs, I was greeted with remarks like "Sleepyhead," and "We thought you were going to sleep all day," but the one that made me look at my watch again was Watson IV's comment that "This place opens to the public at nine, so Mrs. Hudson will need to have the tables cleared and dishes washed by that time."

Mrs. Hudson? She was another character in the Sherlock Holmes stories, but was I supposed to believe that she was Mrs. Hudson IV?

"No," explained Watson IV, "her name is really Anna Wozniakowski. She's from Poland and has lived in London since the war." (I didn't interrupt to ask which war.) "When she applied for the job, we asked if she minded if we called her Mrs. Hudson instead; at first she couldn't understand why, because Wozniakowski was a perfectly good name in the old country, but eventually she consented, and now she has gotten accustomed to being called Mrs. Hudson. And I am sure that you agree that she does a great job making kippers."

I said nothing.

Yes, there was a dog, but it wasn't under my end of the table. It was down at the other end where Samantha was sitting. I should have known. And I managed to down one kipper, or should I say one kip, which I ate with a Danish and a cup of coffee. It seemed odd to enjoy a Danish prepared by a Polish in a British museum.

The next time Mrs. Anna Wozniakowski-Hudson emerged from the kitchen I was officially introduced, although she didn't seem to be thrilled to meet the octogenarian sleuth. As for her, she was, shall I say, rather ordinary, a round-faced little woman with tightly wound grey hair. She was more solid than fat; her wrists were thick and probably her ankles were even thicker, but I didn't dare look down to check.

I heard an "ahem," but I didn't want to wash down the Danish too quickly. It's not good for your digestive system; I think I remember my mother telling me that seventy-some odd years ago. But half of those years were even; only thirty-some were odd.

I ignored the first two ahems, but paid attention when the third ahem was particularized: "Ahem, Pete." Of course, I knew it was Samantha all the time, but sometimes I like to irritate her by not responding to the first ahem. I used to treat my wife the same way.

All I had to say in response was "Where?" which showed Samantha that I was reading her mind and that we were on the same page. I don't think she had any blank pages in her mind, although I carried around a few, some because those pages had been full of things which I eventually erased because I had never referred to in sixty or seventy years. Other pages I wanted to erase but I couldn't; like the fact that Dizzy Dean and his brother Daffy won the pennant for the Cards in 1934 almost single-handedly (or maybe double-handedly.) Anyway, you probably know what I mean, but don't care.

"A little room, back of the gift shop, in five minutes."

It didn't matter that everyone heard where our top-secret meeting was going to be held. They all knew we were working on a high-level case, but only Watson and Roger knew it had something to do with Buckingham Palace, and only Watson himself knew it involved the Queen.

The room was small and musty. Samantha opened the window to bring some fresh air in. The window may not have been lifted since Sherlock Holmes' day. I kept forgetting that Sherlock Holmes was only fictional. I wonder if Watson IV had that problem too.

Samantha had a map of England, a city map of London and the Queen's itinerary during the ten days when she suspected the brooch was lost or stolen.

"She mentioned five places, Pete, and all, except two, have a London address behind their names. But you're the map person, so why don't you tell me where to go today?" She handed me the two maps.

That pleased me for two reasons.

First, she recognized that I was the map person and that she wasn't. Women like people; men like maps. When you are lost, a woman wants to stop at the next corner and ask a stranger who probably just arrived in town himself. A man will bury his head in a map to find out. Either Rand or his partner McNally would know.

Second, I liked the idea that she asked me to tell her where to go. I was going to remember that throughout the day. It might come in handy.

Third, I know I said two reasons, but with Samantha you always have to have a third reason, because she always has one more than you have, and it's wise to get her thinking out before you express your thinking.

"OK, I'm the map guy, and you're the I-phone person. What do you think?"

"We can't waste time, Pete. We've got a lot to do today."

"OK, Samantha, I stand corrected, or right now I'm sitting corrected, so what's the plan?'

A couple of cabbies were honking outside, and when they began yelling at each other, Samantha closed the window. We might suffocate, but at least we could hear each other's last words as we were dying.

"Here's my thinking, but if you don't think it's good, we can change it. You've been in this business a lot longer than I have."

"What's the plan?" Maybe I was being pushy, but I didn't want to suffocate before I knew the plan.

"The only two places on her list that don't have a London address are Sandringham and Elstree. Do you know them, Pete?" She handed me the list which Clarice had printed out for the Queen and which the Queen had given Samantha. The list not only had the name and address of each place but also why each place was famous, no doubt to help the Queen make a short speech when she visited.

I looked down the list quickly and shook my head. "Never heard of them. The last time I was here was forty years ago, and they probably weren't important then."

"Both of them are important to the Queen now, and one of them is very important to me, too."

"Which one?"

"Sandringham."

"What's there?"

"The Royal Stud Farm."

"Oh," I said as if I knew what she was talking about. My mind went as fast as it could without breaking any speed limits—shirt studs, studs in walls, a tire stud, a muscular handsome guy. I didn't want to display my ignorance, so I said, "Let's go there. Who's driving and what is he or she driving?"

"It's between Roger, you and me."

"Let's leave Roger out," I said, "because he shouldn't be 'in the know' about this case."

"I agree, and that leaves you and me. So, which of us has the most experience driving in England?"

"Me."

"Right," she agreed, "but who enjoys driving the most?"

"You."

"Tie score. So who has faster reaction times?"

"I guess you do," I admitted.

"So I win in extra innings. I'm the driver and you're the navigator—though I also have a phone with a GPS that might help. Your friend Watson IV said we could rent a car at the Landmark Hotel in the next block, so what are we waiting for?" When she starts moving, she moves quickly.

She was almost out the door when I said, "I'll tell the others that we'll be gone most of the day, but we'll be back by supper, unless in London they call it dinner, and I'll tell your mum not to worry even though we don't know where we're going." By the time I finished all that, Samantha was nowhere in sight. I guess she didn't hear me.

She heard me. Poking her head back in the still-open door, she said, "But don't tell my mum that I'm driving because that will make her worry for sure.

"OK. Samantha, you run on ahead, and get the car. I'll amble behind as fast as I can amble."

After we climbed into our rental car (I climbed; she hopped), I looked again at Clarice's list of places to investigate. Samantha had also given me a little book that the auto rental people provided with driving tips. Why did I have it? She was the driver, wasn't she? The little book had a lot of stuff about how, where and when to rent a car, which we already knew because we were already on the road and Samantha was trying to find her way out of London.

I also knew that Samantha had found the horn. So I commented, "I don't think they honk their horns here as much as we do in America."

"Is that what it says in that little book?"

"No, it doesn't say a thing about how often one should honk a horn. For all I know, they might call it a bugle in England."

"Then be quiet about it, Pete, and let me drive, unless you want to take over."

"No, we haven't collided with anyone yet, so keep on going. But I've found the section on what Americans need to know about driving in England."

"Good, because we're almost out of London."

"First of all, drive on the left."

She laughed. "That's a good thing to know. What else?"

"Make sure you know how to drive with a manual transmission."

"No problem, Pete. I drive my husband's trucks all the time."

"Watch out for the round-abouts."

"You mean those traffic circles. I went around two of them while you were looking for the right page. In fact, I went around one of them twice."

"Well, then, you know just about everything there is to know."

"Except I'm amazed at the speed limits. We're still in the suburbs and it says I can go sixty miles an hour. There's another sign right up ahead. Look fast, or I'll speed right by it."

I just got a glimpse before she passed it, but then in the deep recesses of my mind I remembered. "Um, Samantha. I don't want to tell you how to drive, but the speed limit is in kilometers, not miles. It's about a five to three ratio."

"You expect me to do geometry when I'm going sixty miles an hour? Why don't they write in English? I was never good in math anyway."

"It's simple, Samantha. If the sign says 100 kph, it really means—let me see now—oh, about sixty miles an hour. You just divide the number by five and multiply by three."

"All right, Pete. Here's a sign that says 48 kph. How fast can I go?"

"Let me find some paper, maybe the back of the rental form. Divide 48 by 5, No, it's easier to add two to 48 and make it 50 and if I divide that by five, I get ten." I was going to write on the back of Clarice's list, but I decided against it.

"Never mind. I'm through that zone. Now, it says resume speed, but I don't remember how fast I was going before."

She managed to find a reasonable speed that matched the traffic around us. It still seemed fast to me, so I buried my head in the little book. After several minutes I looked up. "This is a very helpful book, but if I keep reading it all morning, I'll never wake up and eat the roses."

Samantha laughed. "Pete, you don't eat roses, you smell them."

"Yeah, but maybe I could suggest to Mrs. Hudson that she add some roses to the kippers to make them smell better."

Samantha said we were approaching a town called Bore-hamwood.

"Slow down, Samantha. This is our first stop."

"What do you mean, our first stop? We've hardly got going."

"I know, but part of Borehamwood is called Elstree, or maybe a part of Elstree is called Borehamwood. Anyway, the Queen apparently made a speech here a few weeks ago and it's a possible location for us to investigate."

"What's so special about Elstree?"

"Clarice's list says that the first British films were made here a hundred years ago. So the Queen helped them celebrate the centennial of British film-making. The BBC still makes films here. This is where Judi Dench got her start." We passed signs that designated several studios. It was starting to rain, and in a few seconds, scores of umbrellas went up. Pedestrians all seemed prepared.

"What do I do now?" she asked. It wasn't a big city, but there seemed to be dozens of film studios.

"I don't know. The map doesn't tell me."

She lowered her window and called to a pedestrian she had almost run over. "The centennial celebrations? Where were they held?"

He scratched his chin with one hand while holding onto his umbrella with the other. A car behind ours waited a few seconds before honking. "Oh, yes, the centennial celebrations. In the next square you'll find the Elstree Studio, and I am sure they will know. I'm not completely sure, but I am quite sure that they will know more than I know. If they don't know, try the Neptune Studios in the next square." He resumed his stroll and we hollered our thanks after him.

A gate by the Elstree Studios stopped us. "Purpose of your visit?" the gatekeeper asked. He looked about eighteen.

Samantha looked at me and I said, "Research," as firmly as I could.

"Who will you be seeing?"

I thought a second and said, "The director." I didn't think prime minister or secretary general sounded right, but every film had to have a director.

The gatekeeper seemed apologetic for delaying us. "Not to worry," he explained, "but we've been told to look out for terrorists today. I don't know why they picked today. They should have checked with the weatherman. You don't look like terrorists to me. I have to do my job, you know, but not to worry. Let me see under your bonnet."

Samantha looked at me and raised her eyebrows.

"It's OK," I told her. "He wants to check under the hood."

She turned back to the gatekeeper. "Oh, if that's all you wanted." She looked on the dashboard for the switch to release the hood, but the young gatekeeper seemed more impressed with Samantha than he was in guarding the studio and opened the gate.

"Pardon me, ma'am, but are you a famous actress? If so, I apologize."

"Your apology is accepted," she said quickly without answering his question and she pulled the car into the parking lot.

"Well done," I commented as he waved us through.

At the entrance to the parking lot was a huge sign, "Birthplace of Star Wars." As we came closer to the main entrance there were more signs: "Where Superman Was Really Born," "Sherlock Holmes Lived Here," "Indiana Jones Came from Elstree," "The King's Speech was Delivered Here," "The Shining Dazzled Here," and "Lolita Slept Here."

At the last sign, Samantha asked, "Who was Lolita?"

"Ask your mother," I said quickly.

Another guard inside the door asked our purpose in visiting, and then after eyeing Samantha, he said, "We're not holding any auditions this morning. Maybe this afternoon. You can check in at the casting office over there."

"No, no," I responded. "No one is supposed to know we're here. We were sent by someone very, um, very high up, provided that we keep our visit on the down-low. We just came over early to take a look at your studios here. I wouldn't want Samantha to work in tawdry conditions."

I had no idea what *tawdry* meant, but it seemed very, very bad.

Samantha picked up on it immediately. "We heard that the Queen was here to help you celebrate your centennial. It was a studio where several famous movies were filmed. What studio was it? Do you recall?"

I knew Samantha was winging it. She had no idea what she was talking about, but I think the guard would have given her anything she wanted.

He directed us down the long hall to Studio 6A. As I glanced down the long corridor I realized I should have brought a wheelchair. On the way I asked Samantha, "Have you ever dreamed of becoming a movie star?"

"Of course. Every girl does."

"Really?"

"And my dream role would be to be in a western, to ride a horse all day long and get paid a million dollars a week."

"I didn't think that the money would be such a major attraction for you."

"Not when I was a teenager. Then it was all stardust and moonlight, but now that I am married and have some kids, money matters more."

She went on ahead, while I ambled after her. When we finally walked into Studio 6A, it was impressive. About a hundred big spotlights were hanging from the ceiling, and a dozen cameras were in various places around the room. There was a slightly raised stage area at one end of the big room, and a few risers on the other side, creating an audience area. About thirty chairs were set out, though probably there were more at the gala event. The place seemed like a warehouse, housing equipment until it was next needed somewhere else. I was expecting more of a theater situation, like the time I sat in the back row at a community musical, watching my son play a turtle. I was very proud. But here they were clearly not accustomed to audiences, just cameras. They must have put on some kind of show for the Queen's visit, but now it was all in disarray.

Samantha suggested I sit down and rest a minute while she explored. I tried to visualize where the Queen might have sat, and then I saw two big padded chairs up front, in the center. Surely those were their makeshift thrones, so I went and made myself comfortable. I looked around. The floor was very clean. If the Queen had lost her brooch here, it would have been swept up by the next morning. I'd check later to see if they had a Lost and Found.

But where was Samantha?

I called.

Immediately, she appeared in the back of the stage, pirouetting to the front.

"Not too bad! What didya think, Pete?"

I'm no expert on pirouettes, but I thought it was pretty good, and I gave her a thumbs up. However, before I could say anything, I heard a voice behind me, "In fact, very good."

I turned and saw a rather swarthy man with an unlit cigar sticking out of his mouth. "In fact, this afternoon I am going to be casting for a BBC TV serial, and we have an opening for an American girl who chews gum. You don't happen to chew bubble gum, do you?"

By this time, Samantha had descended from the stage and was standing alongside me. "Oh, I'm so embarrassed. This place is so dark and I didn't know anyone was here."

"Of course, I don't count," I muttered.

"You know what I mean, Pete. I meant anyone important."

The man in the aisle had more to say. "You're perfect, but you didn't answer my question. I asked if you chewed bubble gum."

"I used to, but I gave it up when I got married."

"I happen to have some bubble gum in my pocket," the man continued. "Here." He reached in his pocket and pulled out a stick. "Let me see how long it takes to blow a bubble."

"It's been a while since I've done this," Samantha said nervously. "I'm not sure I can do it anymore." She stuck the gum in her mouth and handed the wrapper to me.

While she was chomping the gum into proper pliability, the man stretched out his hand toward me. "I'm Anthony Cortellini, and I'll be directing a BBC serial to be aired next spring. PBS in the States is very interested, too."

I stood up to shake his hand, but by this time he wasn't paying attention to me; he was watching Samantha.

Samantha's jaws were working hard, and then as she was successfully developing a huge bubble, she waved her arms to get Cortellini's attention—which she already had. Just then the bubble exploded like a pancake all over her face.

Cortellini watched her embarrassment and said to me, "She's perfect."

"But she's not an actress," I protested, a bit worried about what was brewing here. We hadn't come to England to audition; we came to solve the Queen's problem.

"Shush, Pete." Samantha said, using her fingernails to get the gum off her face.

"Rehearsals start next Monday," the director announced.

"But she's not an actress," I repeated.

Cortellini's eyes were still fixed on his new gum-chewer. "I'm not talking to you, sir."

"But you're making a mistake. Samantha's not an actress."

"*Perfectissimo*. She's a natural. You're not her agent, are you?"

"No, I'm just a friend."

Cortellini raised his eyebrows, then looked back at Samantha and repeated, "*Perfectissimo*."

He stuck his unlit cigar back in his pocket, no doubt along with other sticks of gum. I sat down again in the padded chair the Queen had presumably used a few weeks earlier. I shook my head, and silently said, *No, no, no*. But neither Cortellini nor Samantha was paying any attention to me.

By this time he had taken her arm and had led her about twenty feet away, no doubt to talk privately, away from my meddling. I couldn't hear the conversation, but the director raised his voice when he said, "It's your choice, young lady, and not his." He cocked his head in my direction as he said it, and continued talking.

With nothing else to do, I reached down to the floor to see if the Queen's brooch had fallen there. No luck. But as I placed my hand on the chair's padding to shift my weight, I felt something there, something small and spherical. I dug between the chair's cushions and brushed the object with my fingers. I had to get up and bend over to thrust my hand deeper into the cushioned crevice. I'm not sure what this looked like to Samantha and her newfound Lothario, but I didn't care. I was about to crack the case. With one more reach I grabbed the hidden object and pulled it out—a big, round wad of hardened chewing gum. I doubted very much that Queen Elizabeth II was much of a gum-chewer, so I deduced that Anthony Cortellini had been here before.

The Cortellini-Samantha meeting was coming to a conclusion. He had his arm around her waist now as they returned to me.

"Yes, Sammie, you have a future. No money worries forever. In fact, I can see your name in lights already." He took her hand, lifted it to his lips and kissed it.

Samantha was smiling when she returned to me.

We retraced our steps—no, that isn't right, because Samantha was almost skipping and I was ambling more slowly than ever. But as soon as we were out of earshot of that studio, Samantha said, "Anthony really has a line of gab, doesn't he?"

I sighed with some relief. "I thought you were falling for it."

"Maybe I was, a little," she smiled. "I'll tell you more on the way to Sandringham."

But first, we had to stop at the Lost and Found, which the guard directed us to after he asked Samantha, "Did you meet Mr. Cortellini?"

I looked at Samantha and she still had that smile on her face. "Oh, you mean Anthony?" She pulled out a sheet that the director had given her. I saw Cortellini's signature on it.

After she showed it to the guard, he said, "He knows talent when he sees it."

I asked him again about the Lost and Found, and he directed us to the third closet on the right. "Just rummage in it to find what you're looking for. But, sir, I have a better idea. Why don't you stay here at the door? Things are pretty quiet this afternoon. I can help the young lady—did I hear Mr. Cortellini call you Sammie? I like that—Sammie and I can find whatever you're looking for in the closet."

"Thanks, but no thanks," Samantha said quickly. She threaded her arm through mine and said, "Pete knows what to look for."

The Lost and Found had plenty of mittens and umbrellas but no brooches. So we didn't waste time in getting back to the car.

Of course, I was curious about what Cortellini had promised her, but I wasn't overly worried. I trusted Samantha to make good decisions; of course I did. Well, I did sometimes, when we were tracking criminals. But this was different. We were dealing with fame and dreams and spotlights and chewing gum—all uncharted territory for me.

"What's the name of the road to Sandringham?" she asked, snapping me out of my fears. "We're on A-1 now."

"We're looking for A-10, but first we need to find A-25."

"That doesn't make sense. A-1 should be followed by A-2."

"Road-builders don't have to make sense," I declared. "After all, they weren't Rhodes scholars."

Samantha groaned.

CHAPTER 8

S omewhere between Bishop's Stortford and Cambridge, as we were driving on A-10, I finally got her story. It was raining hard now, and I didn't want to take her attention from the road because she had a tendency to straddle the center line.

Straddling the center line made sense to her, she said, because it gave her a choice if another car was coming straight at her. If it was an American car, she would swerve to the right. If it was a foreign car, she would swerve to the left.

"It's worked so far," she said. "Now what was the question you wanted to ask me?"

"Oh, yes. What was it?" I tried to give the impression that I had forgotten it. "Back in the movie studio, you were talking to this director who wanted you to take a part in a BBC television serial."

"Yeah, Pete, but I have to turn him down. After all, what's a few million dollars—or pounds or euros? He kept throwing different kinds of money at me, I couldn't keep up with him."

"You had to turn him down? Why?'

"No, I didn't turn him down yet, but I'm going to."

"Why?" I tried to sound very casual, but I wasn't.

"I guess, Pete, that I would be giving up more than I would get."

"What do you mean?"

"I love my kids too much, and my husband, and my mum and our four dogs. Yeah, I felt I would be giving up more than I would get. You know what I mean."

"Well, I know that you have your head on straight."

"Oh, Pete, you weren't worried that I would fall for his blarney, were you?"

"Just a little."

"And coming from him, it was more baloney than blarney," she laughed. "If he were Irish, it would be blarney."

"Samantha, watch out!" We were suddenly surrounded by a swarm of cyclists.

"Where did they all come from? It's hard enough to drive in the rain with all these guys who don't know what side of the road to drive on, but now we have bicycles, like a swarm of bees."

She slowed down to avoid being crushed by them.

"Must be Cambridge," I said. "I remember it from the time I went here."

"You went to Cambridge, Pete?"

"Of course. I thought you knew that. And I really enjoyed my time here."

"I'm impressed, Pete. What did you study?"

"No, Samantha, I didn't say I *studied* at Cambridge. I said I *went* to Cambridge. For students it takes at least four years, but for motorists, it takes about four minutes."

"Unless a swarm of bicycles slows them down. OK, Pete, but if you went to Cambridge, you should know why it's called Cambridge." "I happen to know that one. We will soon be crossing the river Cam, and so the bridge we will be taking over it is the "Cam-bridge.""

Samantha accepted that, but she didn't want me to have the last correct answer, so she asked, "OK, but can you tell me if London Bridge goes over the London River?"

I was going to answer her question and tell her that the original London Bridge is now in Arizona where rivers are few and far between, but first she started talking about our next stop, Sandringham.

I had to interject, "I suppose it was named for a woman named Sandra who found a ring in the middle of a ham sandwich."

"Sounds like the worst proposal ever," she chuckled.

"Of course ham comes from pigs and Sandringham is known for its horses, not its pigs, right? Didn't you tell me that?"

"Yes," Samantha replied. "That's why Queen Elizabeth visited here. Most of all, Sandringham is known for its stud farm."

"I'm afraid to ask what that is."

"A stud farm," she continued, "is a farm for the selective breeding of livestock. In America, a race horse who wins the Kentucky Derby and a few other big races may be sent to a stud farm and be used to breed future derby winners." Samantha went on, educating me about all the different kinds of horses, and how important breeding is.

"Do they have race tracks here?" I asked, knowing that it would start my partner on another lengthy spiel.

"Of course, but they call it flat racing, and it has its climax in the Royal Ascot, which is the grandest of the grand. Women have to wear hats, so you see some very wild hats displayed. Most of the women are more interested in the hats than they are in the horses, but not Queen Elizabeth. She is certainly interested in the finery, but she is more interested in the horses. At one time she had several stud farms around the country, but now she concentrates on just one: Sandringham. They say that she comes here regularly, so I'm not surprised to see it on our list of places she recently visited.

"When she comes, she watches the horses very carefully, and she knows all about them. Horses and dogs are her passion."

I knew they were Samantha's passion too, so I asked, "Does she breed her dogs here too?"

"Yes, at the Royal Kennel, which, according to the Internet, is next to the Royal Stud Farm. The queen is recognized as an expert in the breeding and training of gun dogs."

"Gun dogs? I bet the NRA is proud of her."

"Don't be silly, Pete. Dogs don't shoot guns."

"I didn't think so. It would be very difficult for a dog to march and carry a rifle at the same time, although some Great Danes might be able to do it. And in the Alps, they have St. Bernards that carry kegs of whiskey around their necks searching for lost mountain climbers. Maybe in England, gun dogs carry pistols around their necks searching for lost bobbies."

"But the bobbies here don't use guns, they use billies."

"Well, I'm glad you straightened me out on that, Samantha, but now watch where you're driving or the bobbies will catch you and you'll have the willies."

Some of our talk was nonsensical, but much of it concerned our strategy of how to search for the Queen's brooch. We planned to separate in Sandringham: she would search for the missing brooch in the Royal Kennels, while I would spend my time looking for the missing piece in the stud farm. But it would be difficult to get much information from the staff without telling them that the queen had sent us, and we couldn't do that.

Samantha and I normally get along famously, but a three-hour drive stretches the best of relationships.

"Oh, Samantha, watch where you're going. You're drifting right!"

"I know, but there was a bicycle on my left."

"Yes, but there was a car on the right!"

"All right, Pete, would you rather drive?" She sounded exasperated, but I knew she would never give up the wheel.

"Well, yes," I said, "but you need the practice, and I can see that you still need more practice, but I must say I'm amazed how well you navigated those traffic circles."

She nodded. "The first two were difficult, I admit. But now I've learned that the best way to get through them is to close your eyes and step on the gas. I learned the technique of navigating traffic circles from watching a movie about a cabbie in Rome. He said that's what he does, and if it works for him in Rome, it should work for me in London."

We didn't say anything for about thirty seconds, and then Samantha said, "Just kidding."

The land was low and flat here; at times it was like Kansas, but with more ditches and marshes. Sometimes it was like Louisiana's bayous, and then suddenly out of nowhere a town would pop up with a magnificent cathedral in the middle. So it was a mix of Kansas and Louisiana with a little bit of Massachusetts thrown in.

When I saw the Ely Cathedral, I had two questions: "How do Brits pronounce Ely?" and "Why did they build it out here in the middle of nowhere a thousand years ago with no McDonald's or Starbucks within fifty kilometers?"

As we approached the village of King's Lynn, I told Samantha, "We're almost there."

"Yeah, I know," she said, "but the road signs are going by so quickly, and the rain smears the windshield so much that I don't have a chance to read them. There's another one coming. I'll slow down so I can read it."

My head was buried in the map, but I felt the car slowing a bit. "It's useless," Samantha griped. "I forget how you told me to convert kilometers into miles, so we're either thirty miles away or five miles away. Not much difference."

Glancing ahead, I saw a bobby standing out in the rain in the middle of the road, halting traffic. Fortunately, Samantha saw him too.

"Oh, oh, what do I do now?"

"First, I'd suggest you stop before you hit him. Maybe they've put out an APB on a reckless driver from America."

As Samantha was slowing to a stop, she said, "Pete, I've forgotten what I did with my driver's license. I hope I didn't leave it in my room. Better have yours handy in case I can't find mine and they lock me up."

"You had to have your license when you rented the car."

"Oh, yeah, I forgot about that. Then it's probably in my purse or with my cell phone or in the glove compartment, one of the three. My purse is probably under the seat. See if you can find it while I talk the bobby out of arresting me."

Samantha was out of the car in the rain as the policeman walked up. I knew Samantha would speak first. She called it her preemptive strike. She always tried to get in both the first word and the last word. "I'm sorry, officer, I mean, bobby, I mean, copper. I'm sorry I did whatever I did." I could tell Samantha was nervous. She always talked rapidly when she was hyper.

"Stand in front of your auto," the officer said in a brisk British accent, "and tell the old man to get out as well. Leave the keys in the ignition."

I tried to get out of the car but I couldn't. No one had instructed me on how to open the passenger's side door. Maybe Samantha had electronically locked the door on my side. Car manufacturers try to make it difficult for kids under eight and seniors over eighty. Every passenger's side door is both different and difficult. They ought to develop a separate manual for that. But I couldn't waste time; the policeman would be asking for Samantha's driver's license any moment now, and she had told me it was probably in her purse under her seat. So I decided to kill two birds with one stone. If I crawled over to the driver's side, I could find her purse and then open *that* door to get out. As I was crawling on the floor boards, I also tried to listen to the animated conversation outside. Samantha was trying to copy a British accent—more specifically to talk as Queen Elizabeth talked.

I managed to find Samantha's purse, but I couldn't find her driver's license. Frankly, I don't know how she could find anything in it. The driver's side door was still partially open, so I knew that if could crawl a foot or two more, I'd be able to get out. I was squished under the steering wheel as the policeman came to open the door where my feet were.

I heard the policeman say, "Begging your pardon, ma'am, are you OK with him? I mean, is he daft or hopeless or helpless?"

And I heard Samantha laugh and say, "A tad of all three."

"Do you want some help with him, ma'am? He won't bite or anything, will he?"

"No, usually he behaves himself quite well."

I knew that the best thing for me to do was to play dumb and be dumb until Samantha got away from this officer, but the gear shift was sticking in my ribs, so I had to do something.

"There's a line of cars waiting, so I have to leave you, ma'am. Best of luck in Sandringham."

A minute later, the officer had left and I was wrenching my stomach away from the gear shift, still holding onto Samantha's purse.

I looked up and saw her laughing. "What were you doing down there, Pete?"

"You told me your driver's license might be in your purse."

"Well, I hope that you didn't mess it up. I spent a half hour last night getting it organized."

"Didn't the policeman ask for your driver's license?"

"Yes, at first, but then I told him that I was going to Sandringham to see the royal Clydesdales, and I was talking so fast in my fake British accent that he couldn't understand me and I think he thought I was the Duchess of Clydesdale, going to Sandringham to buy a horse for my estate."

"Duchess of Clydesdale? Is there such a person?"

"I don't know, but he thinks there is, and that's all that counts."

"Does that make me a duke?" I suggested.

"No. I said you were my driver. So maybe you'd better take the wheel until we get to Sandringham."

When things happen fast like this, it is hard for me to know what emotions I should summon. Later, I might think it all through slowly and decide whether to be angry or not. But now I just walked around, got into the driver's seat, said, "Yes, your Highness," and started the car.

After we got back on the road, I wondered aloud, "So why was he stopping traffic?"

"They had a tip about some 'trouble' in the area. He wouldn't say any more, just told me to be careful. I mentioned that you used to be an MP, and he shook his head and said, 'That explains it.'"

"Of course, in England an M.P. is a member of Parliament, and half of England thinks the whole government is crazy."

"But it isn't a lie, Pete, because you really were a Military Policeman sixty years ago."

"And don't you forget it," I warned.

"I felt bad about confusing him. I'm surprised my British accent could fool anybody. I think I picked it up from watching 'Upstairs, Downstairs.'"

I glanced over at Samantha. "You know, you're pretty clever."

"I think that's the first nice thing you've said to me on this entire trip."

"OK. Here's something else for you. Before I got down and started crawling around on the floorboards, I saw you standing out front with that bobby, and I thought how great you looked, but then I wondered whether you should be wearing that dress on a day when we're visiting a dog kennel and a horse stable."

"You like the dress, Pete? My mum bought it for me two days ago. The color is royal purple, and my mum said that if I didn't like it she would wear it."

"I like the style, though I'm not sure I would wear it to a kennel."

"For your information, Pete, it's called an empire gown, and also for your information, you are not the one who is wearing it to a kennel; I am. And also for your information, I have a change of clothes in the trunk, just in case I have a chance to ride a horse at the stud farm."

We were approaching another roadblock; I braked slowly.

"Hmm," said Samantha. "Maybe these are the 'troubles' Walter was talking about. Looks like they're fixing potholes. I thought he was talking about, like, terrorists."

"Walter?"

"The bobby who stopped us before. He was very nice."

"Of course."

One of the workmen pointed me to a single lane on the opposite side of the road. The workers were repaving a section of it, so we had to wait a half minute for a southbound auto to get by before we could proceed.

"But maybe . . ." I could tell the gears in Samantha's brain were whirring away with a new idea. She turned in the passenger seat to face me. "What if this road work is just a trick? Maybe there really *are* terrorists, and the police are using this road crew to slow them down."

"What would your close personal friend Walter say about that?"

She folded her arms. "I don't know. Maybe the same as your close personal friend Ariana."

"I thought you weren't going to mention her on this trip."

"Just fighting fire with fire. Besides Walter never invited me to go to Paris."

"I'm not going to Paris with Ariana!" I insisted.

"Could be nice," she said with a tight smile. "I'm just saying."

The workman was waving us through, and as we proceeded I saw several police cars along the road. "Maybe you're right, Samantha. There seems to be a lot of police interest in these potholes. But I can't imagine why terrorists would want to terrorize Sandringham."

"Oh, I hope they don't hurt the animals."

"I was a bit more worried about *us*."

I drove on slowly, perhaps too slowly, judging by the number of cars that were passing us. I was trying to keep an eye out for potential terrorists, but I also remembered my great-grandmother saying that it is better to be safe than sorry. I hoped that Samantha would take note of how carefully I was driving.

But after a few more kilometers, there was another road-block, this one with no road crews around, just police. As we stopped, I noticed that cars ahead of us were searched carefully: The passengers had to get out as the boots (trunks), the bonnets (hoods), the wings (fenders), and even underneath the car were searched.

When I rolled down the window, the royal policeman came and made a semi-bow in Samantha's direction. And then, talking past me toward the duchess, "Apparently, it is still safe, Ma'am. No real trouble yet. Sorry for the delay, but better safe than sorry." He didn't credit my great-grandmother, but I wasn't aware that her saying was known even in England.

Samantha replied to the policeman in her best regal voice, "You mean that no terrorists have been spotted, but I suppose you have been picking up chatter on the web." I glanced admiringly at my partner. Where had she learned to speak like that? The citizens of Clydesdale could be proud of their crime-fighting duchess now.

"All day, my lady, but no activity yet. We're not supposed to talk about it, but I suppose Walter clued you in. He radioed ahead and asked me to keep an eye out for you. I hope we haven't caused any inconvenience."

"No more than necessary, I'm sure," said Samantha with a sweet smile that seemed to melt the policeman.

"You may proceed then, but it would behoove you not to abide in Sandringham for more than an hour and certainly not into the vesper hours."

Never in my life had I heard a policeman use the words *behoove* and *vesper* before. I think he was telling us to get moving, get there, and get out, but it sounded nicer the way he said it.

We drove quietly for the next few minutes, looking for signs to the kennels and stud farm. Then Samantha spoke: "You know, Pete, it's not that I'm afraid or anything like that, but I think we ought to stay together, in case we need to leave quickly."

"What do you mean?"

"I don't know. It's just a funny feeling I have."

Then came the sign to the kennels. The parking area was large, but almost empty, so, as the chauffeur, I drove close to the kennels and let the duchess dismount near the entrance. "Pete, you don't have to open the passenger's side door for me. I can open it all by myself—unlike other people I know."

I watched as she walked very properly to the entrance, talked to someone and then went in. Before I parked, I wanted to make sure the bobbies hadn't closed the place. Perhaps it was only a potential terrorist threat, and maybe the Brits are more accustomed to such threats than Americans are, but I didn't know why this place was still receiving visitors—though I was glad it was. I parked and ambled back to the entrance. Inside, I found Samantha listening to a taped lecture on the care and feeding of Gun Dogs.

When she saw me, she said, "This place is in good order too, but let's prowl around for a few minutes and see if we can find anything that has been overlooked. If a brooch had fallen here, someone would have found it by this time. Pete, let's meet back here again in ten minutes, OK?"

I had hardly gotten fifty feet away when I heard her yell, "Pete, come here, fast."

I ambled back to her in double-time. She was pointing at a little pile of soot and droppings that the cleaning people had apparently forgotten to pick up.

"Pete, see this?" She was excited. "Don't touch anything. This mess must have been put here only a few minutes ago. Everything else is spotless."

I looked at it more carefully. I didn't see the brooch. All I saw was a pile of soot surrounding a cigarette butt and a woman's lipstick container.

"That's lipstick, not a brooch, Samantha," I said, though I was aware she knew more about lipstick than I did.

"It isn't lipstick, Pete; it's an SCR."

"A what?"

"A silicon controlled rectifier, and it contains a small digital timer. As soon as a janitor comes to sweep up this corner, the SCR will be activated and it will digitally activate one or two others nearby, maybe one in the Royal Stables."

"Are you sure?"

"Yes, I'm sure. I studied this in college. I even tried to make one at home. It's not hard to do, but my husband stopped me because he didn't want the place incinerated."

"If I understand this right, Samantha, someone could activate this device at any time."

"Right, Pete, and that's why we have to get word to the police as soon as possible."

"You go ahead, Samantha. You understand it, so you can explain it to the bobbies better than I can. I'll stay here and make sure that no one tries to clean up this mess."

As soon as she left, I knew it was a mistake. If someone at the Royal Stud Farm next door disturbed *their* SCR accidentally, it would activate all the SCRs in the area and incinerate anyone who was dumb enough to stand nearby, like me. I took two steps back, hoping that might give me a tenth of a second more to react.

And then in the distance I heard the distinctive high frequency wah-wah-wah of a British siren. Something was happening. Maybe somebody had discovered something. I knew Samantha had discovered this device in the Royal Kennels. Had someone discovered another one elsewhere?

I heard the dogs yelping. No, they weren't yelping; they were wailing. Their ears had picked up the siren before mine did. According to Samantha, they kept only about twenty dogs here, but it sounded like a hundred.

Across the long corridor that led to the entrance (and hopefully an exit), I saw Samantha talking to a guard. Then the guard was motioning outside to summon a bobby.

The sirens finally stopped; and the dogs gradually stopped wailing.

Samantha, the guard, and the bobby were having an animated conversation. Beyond them a car—a police car—squealed to a stop; two officers jumped out and surrounded Samantha. Then Samantha was pointing back to the trash behind me, or else she was pointing at me, and all five of them—the two Royal police officers, the local bobby, the kennel guard and Samantha—came rushing toward me. I thought they would go beyond me to find the SCR in the trash. But they stopped when they got to me.

"In the name of the Queen, I arrest both of you for terrorism, intended murder and unspeakable crimes against the British empire and humanity at large."

"What are you talking about?" I asked in protest.

"It would be wise for you to keep your counsel until you have a barrister," said one officer loudly into my ear as if I were completely deaf.

I couldn't believe it. Samantha was shaking her head as if she couldn't understand it either. But I had to protest some more. "Didn't Samantha tell you about the explosive we discovered?"

"Or the explosives that you planted," responded one officer. Another officer announced loudly so that everyone in the whole area could hear: "Among other heinous crimes, you will be charged with bringing explosives into Royal facilities in an attempt to demolish those facilities, you will be charged with identity theft and impersonating royalty as well as you, sir, falsely presenting yourself as an elected member of Parliament."

The local bobby had his hand around Samantha's wrist, while she vainly struggled to free herself. She had always found it difficult to talk without using her hands. Finally, she freed herself enough to say, "But sir, I don't care what you do to us; I just don't want those precious dogs to be incinerated too."

I'm not sure I agreed with her priorities, but it didn't matter. Her plea didn't reach their ears.

The Scotland Yard officer said to his sergeant, "Search them and make sure they have no trigger for the explosives. Then take them out to the patrol car and cage them in. I'll be with you as soon as I make some phone calls. Scotland Yard will be expecting them."

The local police officer was looking through Samantha's purse. "Look what I found in her purse, Chief. A bloody list of all the places they plan to bomb next. At the top of the list are the Stables and the Stud Farm. You better alert the Yard about these other places. These blokes might be the ringleaders of a whole gang of bloody terrorists."

I ran out of things to say, but Samantha was still trying to talk some sense to these policemen. "If someone comes to clean up that mess in the corner, both these buildings will go up in smoke."

"I don't think so, lady; our demolition crew will be coming through the door at any minute, and they'll take care of it. Right now, you two are going to have a little ride back to London. And on the way you can think about whether you want to open up and confess or not. Those Scotland Yard blokes can be pretty rough, and even on pretty young ladies, who might not be so pretty after a few days in a prison cell with a few older and more experienced women who enjoy initiating girls like you into the realities of prison life."

CHAPTER 9

On the outskirts of King's Lynn, Chief Brookings finally paused in his interrogation. He was driving the police van at about 100 kilowatts or whatever and asking questions at the same time. Samantha and I were in the back, enclosed in a steel cage like wild animals. The side windows were blackened, so we couldn't see out. When we answered the chief, he would repeat our answers on the radio for the benefit of Sergeant Wilde, who was somewhere behind us, driving our rental car back to London, and also for the benefit of Scotland Yard, listening in from headquarters. It was an ingenious three-way communication system.

They thought they had caught us "in the act." I was the ringleader, *il capo,* though somewhat senile, and Samantha was a foot soldier in the mob. Many of their questions were directed to Samantha, probably because they thought she would crack under repeated questioning. We claimed we were tourists: Samantha had a list of five places we were planning to visit, but except for St. Paul's Cathedral in London, these were not typical tourist attractions. For instance, what typical tourist would have the Great Western Hospital in Wiltshire in his or her travel plans? And why would anyone care to visit the Chelsea Flower Show a month after it closed?

They admitted that we didn't seem to be the typical terrorists. On the other hand, we weren't the typical tourists either. Many things didn't make sense to them. We could have clarified matters easily, but we had pledged our secrecy to the Queen. It would have been easy if we could say, "Why don't you ask Queen Elizabeth II about us. She will tell you." But we couldn't do that.

At one point, Samantha said, "I've never ridden in a paddy wagon before."

I knew the Chief could hear us, but he let us talk in the hopes that he would pick up some incriminating information.

So I answered, "No, Samantha, in England they don't call them paddy wagons. We are riding in a police van. Right, chief?" I was hoping to start a civil conversation with the police chief even though he had us caged.

"Right," he answered quickly. "They are called paddy wagons in America—I think it was in Boston because most of the police there were Irish. Or else it was because they were picking up so many drunks in the Irish section of town." Then he became suddenly aware that his intercom had not been turned off: "Scotland Yard officers, I apologize if any of you have come from the Emerald Isle. Now let's get back to business."

His interrogation continued as he resumed his driving speed.

Chief Brookings: *Where are you staying in London?*

Samantha: *At the Sherlock Holmes Museum on Baker Street.*

Brookings: *You're lying. Give me the truth. OK, old man, I'll ask you, Where did you sleep last night?*

Pete: *Same as Samantha.*

Brookings: *You slept together,*

Samantha: *Oh, no, sir. I slept with my mother. And Pete slept with the director of the museum.*

Brookings: *With your mother? Does your mother know what you and Pete are involved in?*

Samantha: *Oh, no, sir. She's completely innocent. And sometimes, I don't even know what's going on myself until Pete tells me.*

Brookings: *Just what we thought. OK, Pete, what do you have to say to all this. Your accomplice has just admitted that you plan these attacks.*

Pete: *You don't understand, sir. I don't plan any attacks. This is all make- believe.*

Brookings: *At the Royal Kennels those weren't make-believe bombs. Those were real. And you could have been charged with first degree murder if we hadn't called in the bomb squad just in time.*

Samantha: *Were the bombs defused?*

Brookings: *Yes, I just heard that the master SCR was in the stud farm and our men defused it with only five minutes to spare.*

Samantha: *Awesome! Isn't that beautiful, Pete?*

Brookings: *Stop it. You're confusing me! You planted those bombs, didn't you?*

Pete: *No, officer, Samantha didn't plant them; she discovered them, and when you came into the kennels, she showed them to you. She had shown them to the guard at the kennels just a minute before you arrived. She's the hero, not the villain.*

Brookings: *A likely story. Yard, were you able to copy all of that nonsense?*

I couldn't tell if the Yard copied us or not, because the communications were interrupted by a series of beeps. And then this: "Attention, all officers near Ely on A10. A black Fiat crashed through a roadblock north of Kings Lynn, injuring the officer on duty, and is now heading high speed near Downham."

Brookings answered immediately: "I read you, Yard. Are you there, Sergeant Wilde?"

"Yes, Chief, probably three or four minutes behind you. A black Fiat tore past me about ten seconds ago, Chief. I couldn't even see his number plate."

"Yard, see if you can get a Cambridge patrolman at that round-about where A14 comes through just above Cambridge."

"Will do" came the voice on the intercom.

Samantha tugged on my shirt sleeve and whispered, "I hope it wasn't Walter."

Brookings must have overheard, "Who are you talking about?"

I tried to explain. "Walter was the patrolman at the first roadblock after King's Lynn He was the guy who called Samantha the Duchess of Clydesdale."

Samantha wanted to do more explaining: "I guess I was talking too fast for him. I talk fast when I get excited. I told him I wanted to go to the Stud Farm to see the Clydesdale horses."

I heard a few oh's over the intercom, so I continued: "And he must have thought Samantha said something about being the Clydesdale duchess.

Samantha motioned to the intercom and I nodded. We had a bigger audience than Chief Brookings, so she added: "Then he said he would radio ahead to tell them that the Duchess of Clydesdale was coming. I guess he called ahead. But I liked Walter. I don't want him to be hurt by a crazy hit-and-run driver."

Chief Brookings wasn't listening. Despite the rain, he was on his way south at a rapid clip. Suddenly he yelled, "Keep your bloody heads down; the black Fiat is coming up behind us fast, very fast."

Two shots caromed off the police car as the terrorists raced by.

"Ouch," Samantha said.

I knew she wasn't hit, but I grabbed her hand anyway. I wasn't afraid, of course—well, maybe just a little bit, but I thought Samantha might be a lot.

"Stay low," I whispered to her. I don't know why I was whispering

"We'll catch them," Chief Brookings said. "But I don't know how. When this buggy goes more than a hundred it has convulsions. I hope we have someone at the round-about."

I whispered a translation for Samantha, "He is saying that when he tries to go faster than sixty, the car feels like it's falling apart."

"I know, Pete. I can understand English." Then to Brookings she asked, "Are you OK, chief?" She was still in her crouched position, but she pulled her hand away from mine so she could talk better. She always needed two hands to talk.

"Glad these vans are bullet-proof," I commented to the front seat.

"So am I," said Brookings. "The newer ones are; this is an old one."

We poked our heads up again so we could see what was happening out the front windows.

The intercom was blaring again. "This is the Yard, Brookings. What's the damage? We could hear gunfire."

Brookings answered quickly, "All OK here. Those guys must be going 140 kph, and they are armed and dangerous. Warn the men at Cambridge. My prisoners are OK too. A little shaken up, but that's the fault of this old van just as much as the gunfire."

A moment of silence followed and then the intercom came on again. "By the way, Chief Brookings, the story that your prisoners gave you checks out. The Holmes Museum director says they are legit; they're detectives from the States and are tracking down a case here. They may be an odd couple, but you can release them any time you want."

I decided to speak up. "Thank you, Yard," I said to the unknown voices on the other end of the intercom, "but if the chief doesn't mind, Samantha and I would like to stay in the cage for a few more minutes."

The chief responded, "Good decision. Those blokes don't have any manners. They're shooting bloody bullets."

I remembered the comments of Samantha's mother that our detective work in England would be safer because the police use billy clubs. But I hoped that Chief Brookings had more than a billy club to use with the terrorists. The fact that he didn't fire back when the Fiat passed him made me doubt that he was armed.

Ahead we could see the roadblock at the round-about before Cambridge. The local bobbies were blocking the way, but the terrorists had them backing up. We heard gunfire as we approached.

When we pulled to a stop right behind the terrorists' auto, the chief said to me without turning around, "Pete, I'm getting out, but don't let these terrorists take this van."

I looked at Samantha and found her looking quizzically at me, wondering how we were supposed to stop the terrorists when we were still locked in the back cage.

Brookings added: "The Yard has probably dispatched reinforcements from London already, but it'll take a half-hour to forty-five minutes for them to arrive, so if they put me down, try to delay them a little."

Frankly, my opinion of the chief wasn't too high as he was driving the van, but when he got out and began walking to the scene of the action, he looked seven feet tall. Soon he was standing between the terrorists and the Cambridge bobbies.

All Samantha could think to say was, "Wow! He's a cool cat."

"Yeah," I agreed.

We could hear some of the conversation, but we craned our necks to look through the van's windshield and get in on the video as well as the audio.

"Put down your weapons." I heard him say. "I am the chief of police here and I command you to drop your weapons immediately or else."

The terrorists smirked at each other. One asked, "Or else what?"

"They're laughing at him," Samantha commented.

One of the terrorists waved his arm, "If any of you pasty-faced bobbies want to stay alive and keep your heads on your shoulders, open up a path for our car to get through."

Neither the Cambridge bobbies nor Chief Brookings moved, but one of the terrorists pulled out a weapon and fired; a local bobby fell to the ground.

"We've gotta do something, Pete!" Samantha tried to climb into the front seat, but she couldn't; we were still confined to our cage. She looked at me again and said, "We can't allow the cops to get beheaded." She was determined to break out.

"Wait." I said, pulling her shoulders back to the seat again. "There's another car pulling up." I could see it in the rear-view mirror. "It's your rental car, Samantha."

"It must be Sergeant Wilde."

"I think you're right."

"I hope they don't ding it up."

The terrorists as well as the police officers were looking in our direction and at the new officer advancing on the scene.

"Do you think they can see us?" she asked.

"I don't think so. But even if they do, it doesn't matter."

One of the terrorists shouted, "Put your hands in the air." He spoke in perfect English, so probably the terrorists came from a terror cell in London. All the British officers had upraised arms and Sergeant Wilde joined the group with his hands up in the air.

But while everyone was looking at Sergeant Wilde, I glanced at Chief Brookings. He stuck one hand in his pocket and pulled out a pistol, aiming it at the terrorists. "Hey, look at the chief, Samantha. I didn't know he had a gun."

"I didn't know it was allowed," she responded.

We heard the pop. One of the terrorists went down on his knees, his weapon falling to the ground. The other terrorist reached for his own gun and started shooting wildly. One bullet caromed off our windshield. I didn't know what he was aiming at. But it gave the chief time to aim his gun at Terrorist Number Two and now he was down on the ground too.

I looked over toward Samantha. She had a big smile on her face. "Let me explain it to you, Pete. What the chief has is not a regular weapon. It's a stun gun that paralyzes the victim but doesn't kill him."

Of course, she was right. Sometimes she can act as if she doesn't know anything, but when it's crunch time, she is on top of the situation.

I began to hear some radio static. "The chief didn't turn off his intercom, Samantha. Scotland Yard has heard everything. What a hero Chief Brookings turned out to be."

"And now," Samantha reported loud enough for the intercom, "Chief Brookings is bringing all the bad guys over here. I hope they don't try to squeeze them into this cage with us."

It didn't quite happen that way. Instead, the chief unlocked our backseat cage to let us out first, and then shoved the bad guys in to take our places. Sergeant Wilde gave me the car keys, which I passed along to Samantha as my designated driver.

After starting the car, she asked, "Does Cambridge have a Starbucks? You ought to know. You went there."

Believe it or not, we found a Starbucks in Cambridge, which I suppose isn't surprising in a college town. We were still shaking so much we could hardly handle our cups of coffee. The coffee was too hot anyway. I blew on mine to cool it. Samantha was the first to speak.

"Well, Pete, what have we accomplished today?"

I hate it when the question is asked like that. It reminds me of when my dad used to ask me at the supper table, "What did you learn in school today?" But at that point I wasn't thinking of my dad or even of Samantha, but rather of the Queen, so I had to answer "Not much," which is also the answer I usually gave my dad.

Then I added quickly, "But you, Samantha, saved the Stud Farm and the Royal Kennels from disaster; I don't think anyone will ever know about that, including Queen Elizabeth."

Samantha agreed with my "not much" evaluation and then thought she should phone her mum to tell her we were OK, but that we might be a little late for supper on account of, you know, terrorists. After the mother-daughter conversation had ended, which was just a second after I had reminded her that her coffee was getting cold, Watson IV got on the line.

"Let me step into my office, Pete. It's a little noisy out here."

So ten seconds later he continued, "Just got a call from Clarice—you know who she is?"

"Oh, yes, I know Clar—ICE, and Samantha knows her even better." My partner wrinkled her brow at me, wondering what this was all about.

"I didn't understand it," continued Watson, "but the Queen is apparently upset. Something about terrorists at Cambridge, and something about you two being heroes again. The Queen told Clarice that she hadn't brought you here to be heroes. You'll have to explain it to me when you get here. Anyway, Pete, Clarice wants you or Samantha to phone her."

"It'll be Samantha," I responded.

After we said goodbye or Ta-ta or maybe just Ta to Watson IV, we sat sipping our coffee, looking at each other and trying to calm down. Samantha still found it difficult to bring her cup to her lips without spilling, and I bent over poured some coffee into the saucer and sipped. I wouldn't do it in public, of course, but I thought Cambridge students probably did it all the time. Oxford would probably be different.

We were quiet all the way back. It had started raining again as A10 bypassed the town of Ware. The sign said thirty kilometers to London. I didn't know if that meant to the city limits, to Piccadilly or to Big Ben, but it really didn't matter. We were almost there and with Samantha at the wheel, the car, in spite of the rain, was chewing up the kilometers quite rapidly.

We talked about what we would investigate tomorrow, and I asked, "What's the last one on your list?"

"Chief Brookings confiscated my list as evidence, but don't worry, I had it memorized. Why do you ask about number five?"

"Well, after reading mystery stories all my life, I have come to the conclusion that the correct answer is always the last one. So if the detective played it smart, he would investigate the last possibility first. You know, the one that comes just before the last page of the book."

Then Samantha's cell phone buzzed again. She picked it up, glanced at it, and said, "It's Watson IV again. Should I answer it?"

I was going to say no, but before I could get the word out, Samantha said, "Maybe they want us to pick up a loaf of bread on the way home." So she answered, "Hi, Dr. Watson, I'm giving the phone to Pete. I've got to concentrate on my driving. It's raining pretty hard here."

So I took the phone and asked, "What can we do for you, John?"

"For the last fifteen minutes the media has been camped on our front steps and pounding on our front doors."

"Who did you say was camped on your front steps and pounding on your doors?"

"The media—the papers and the BBC—they all want to interview you. I guess we can hold them off a few minutes more. Roger will be waiting at the hotel where you rented your auto. He'll have some umbrellas for you and will show you a back entrance to avoid the media. And you should also know that I received another call from Clarice. She emphasized that the Queen isn't at all pleased about the publicity you two are receiving. So one of you had better call her as soon as you can."

"OK, John. As soon as you turn off the rain, Samantha will make the call."

Samantha nodded in my direction and mouthed the word *Good.*

In a few minutes we were in London and I was guiding Samantha from A10 across the city to Holborn, to Oxford St. and at last to Baker St. It would have been easier if the streets in London didn't change their names every quarter-mile or so.

It was still pouring when Samantha pulled the rental auto to the front of the hotel.

"Pete, check with the doorman and find out where I should return the car. Then find Roger. No sense both of us getting soaked."

"I'll wait inside."

The doorman, carrying his own umbrella, was already coming to talk to Samantha, so I went inside and found Roger, who gave me two umbrellas and the directions to the back entrance of the museum.

"Ready to talk to the media?" he asked with a smile.

"I have two speeches prepared," I answered, "and I don't know which one to give."

He laughed, thinking I was joking, but it was true. I was always prepared with two speeches. The first was "No comment," and the second, "I plead the Fifth." Here in London I wasn't sure if the second would work

Before Roger left for the museum, I told him it would be ten or fifteen minutes before we would get back. Not only did Samantha have to return the auto but she also had to phone Clarice at Buckingham Palace.

It took even longer than that because they found a hole in the wing, and my first reaction was, "you weren't flying that low." But Samantha said the rental man explained to her that what we call fenders they call wings.

"It's more than a ding or a dent, Pete; it's hole, a bullet hole."

"It must have happened when Sergeant Wilde had the car."

"Yeah, probably. Do you think Scotland Yard will reimburse us?"

"It might be easier to get a few extra quid from the Queen," I said.

"A quid? What's that?"

"I'm not sure. I think it's British slang for money."

"Anyway, you just reminded me to phone Clarice. I hope they don't keep banker's hours at Buckingham."

"Remember," I cautioned, "we don't know if Clarice knows anything about the details of the case."

"Yeah, I know I've got to watch what I say, but today has been so complicated that it will be hard to tell Clarice anything without telling her everything."

Just as she started to call Buckingham on her cell phone, I interrupted. "Samantha, I think it would be good if Clar-ice could set up a short appointment for us with the Queen tomorrow morning. It would be best if we could try to explain things to the Queen in person."

She nodded and said, "I'll try."

I tried to eavesdrop or ears-drop, but I gave up after a few seconds and decided to work on a third speech for the media in case neither of the first two speeches would satisfy them.

"Unaccustomed as I am to public speaking . . ." I memorized that quickly and I thought that would be a good start, but then I was stumped on what I should say next. I had barely memorized those immortal words before Samantha had finished her call.

I looked at my crime-fighting partner and said, "Well-ll-ll-ll?"

"All she said was that the Queen wasn't happy."

"I knew that much."

"And that we had spoiled the reason why she came to us in the first place."

"She didn't care that we had risked our lives to save her kennels and the Royal Stud?" I thought if I said it that way it would sound more dramatic.

"She didn't say anything about that."

"Did she say whether or not we could have an audience with the Queen tomorrow to explain things?"

"The Queen has now retired for the night, according to Clarice, but she will ask her again the first thing tomorrow and call us immediately if there's an opening on her schedule."

"Doesn't sound good, does it?"

"No, it doesn't, but Pete, I consider Clarice a friend, and you might think her name rhymes with *ice*, but it also rhymes with *nice*."

With that bit of Pollyanna sentiment, I put an umbrella into her hand and said, "Let's brave the rain."

And as we stepped outside she said, "The rine in Spine sties mine-ly on the pline." I responded with "The ice in Clar-ice fits nicely with the Queen."

"Oh, Pete, stop it. Be positive."

"Yes, I like to be positive when it's at all realistic."

We said nothing the rest of the way. I ambled as quickly as I could. She was always four steps ahead of me, but then she glanced back, even though she was peeved with me, to see whether or not I had slipped and fallen in the gutter. She was thoughtful that way.

Roger told me the foolproof way of finding the museum's back door in pouring rain. It's the fourth door in from the corner and it has five steps before the landing. I couldn't do many more than five steps at a time especially when holding an umbrella in my right hand and holding a railing with my left. Samantha was ahead of me as usual.

Inside, we sat as close to the fire as we could. It may have been the same one that Sherlock Holmes had enjoyed—no, not the fire, but the fireplace, and not the fireplace either, because Sherlock was only fictional, and we were real, at least we thought we were.

Mrs. Hudson was a little disgruntled about warming up the food. "It's only perfect the first time. I might as well start all over again." But she didn't. We ate leftovers, and they were good.

Shirley and John Watson IV asked questions, and we answered what we could very carefully. As we were talking, we could hear reporters outside in the rain waiting for us to come out for some kind of press conference. One reporter was bold enough to climb up and peek through a window.

"It looks as if they won't disperse until one of you goes out and gives them a scoop or something," Watson said.

Samantha shook her head, turned to me, and said, "Don't do it, Pete."

But I had to. Years ago I was a newspaperman for a short time, and I felt sorry for those guys out in the rain. Besides that, I had three speeches already memorized—at least three speeches partially memorized.

So I said, mostly to Samantha, "I've got to, for old time's sake." And I pulled on a wet jacket and opened the front door. Flashes went off, blinding me for a second. I had forgotten they would be taking pictures. Despite the photos, I remembered my first speech: "No comment." I said the words flawlessly and I returned inside, rather proud of myself, although I wished I hadn't been photographed.

When the clamor didn't stop, I went back outside again and said, "As an American, I am pleading the second amendment, or was it the twelfth, maybe the fifteenth. Anyway, I am pleading one of those amendments." And then I made a quick amble back inside the museum again, slightly embarrassed that I had forgotten which amendment to plead.

When the continuing din outside compelled me to return to the front porch again, it was like a third encore. I had to finish it off this time. So I went out and recited my memorized speech: "Unaccustomed as I am to public speaking," but then my mind went blank. What was I going to say next? Never at a loss for

words, I said, "I want to thank all of you for coming out on this rainy afternoon. I know you must have many other things you would rather do, so I suggest you go home and do them. I also need to explain that I have an ailment which is common to gentlemen my age and even to men who are not really gentlemen at all. In professional circles it's called STMD—"short term memory dysfunction." To put it in laymen's terms, I don't remember what happened today. Thank you and good night."

Inside, the fire in the fireplace was dying out. Mrs. Hudson was trying to be graceful about it as she shooed everyone to his or her own room.

As the others were going upstairs, Samantha motioned me to wait behind, so she and I stood at the bottom of the staircase. Then she spoke softly and soberly, "Pete, you shouldn't have done that."

"Did I say something wrong?"

"No, it wasn't what you said, but what you did. Now every paper in the country will have your picture. The queen wants us to be anonymous. But we are anonymous no longer. I wouldn't be surprised if she fires us on the spot. Or probably she will ask Clarice to do the dirty work. However, in the unlikely chance that she is willing to see us again, we have to come up with a plan so dramatic that it will blow her away. It's got to be truly awesome."

"I'll try, but for some reason I don't feel truly awesome tonight."

CHAPTER 10

"**M**rs. Hudson's morning coffee will put steel in your spine, Pete."

I looked up at Watson IV to see whether or not he was kidding, and then I looked at the cup of coffee in front of me at the breakfast table. Both gave me the same message; he wasn't kidding. Maybe that's what I needed—some steel in my spine. A couple toothpicks to prop my eyes open might help also.

I hadn't slept much last night. It seemed that every move I had made yesterday afternoon and evening was a disaster as far as our royal mission for Queen Elizabeth was concerned.

I sipped at the coffee twice. The slag from the steel mills caught in my throat. I put a teaspoon of sugar in it, then another, then a third. When I reached for water to wash down the steel splinters, Mrs. Hudson was there, filling my cup to the brim. "Gut, vasn't it?"

The phone rang. Watson IV had an answering service that handled most of the calls for the museum, but he had a private line for personal calls. He rose and went to his office immediately. Then a few seconds later, he called out, "Samantha, it is for you."

Then as he was coming out of his office and Samantha was entering, I saw him mouthing the name, "Clarice," and I saw her nodding.

I might as well pack my bags right now for our return trip to America, I thought.

Samantha's phone conversation with Clarice didn't last long. I hadn't expected it to. As she emerged from the office, she summoned both Watson and me inside. She asked, "When the Queen says, 'Immediately,' how long does she mean?"

"Well, she is known to be very impatient," Watson replied, "so her 'immediately' means as soon as possible, if not sooner."

"And how long will it take Roger to drive us to Buckingham?"

"If he were here, fifteen minutes, but he is on an errand this morning."

"All right, John, how long will it take *you* to drive us to Buckingham?"

Samantha was running the show now.

John Watson IV was sputtering no. I didn't know if it was because he didn't have a driver's license or whether it was beneath him as an Oxford professor to become a chauffeur. "It's almost time for the museum to open, and I need to be here to open it."

Samantha was like a bulldog; she wouldn't let go. "My mother is very capable; she has done almost everything there is to do in the world; I am sure she can run a museum for thirty minutes if the Queen wants to see her daughter immediately. Now I need to talk to Pete for a minute in private."

I was never surprised by Samantha. No, that isn't quite true. I was always surprised by Samantha. She could change roles and moods at the drop of a hat.

When the office door was closed, she asked me, "In your sleepless night, was your thinking any more productive than mine?"

"I doubt it, but I knew we needed to do two things today, so I concentrated on one of them. I knew that if I didn't disguise myself, the media would be dogging our steps the whole day; we also needed to find the queen's brooch, but I thought you could worry about that one."

"OK, what did you come up with for a disguise?"

"I thought I would disguise myself as an old man."

Samantha stared at me. "Pete, I hate to break the news to you, but you *are* an old man. You've been an octogenarian longer than I've been a twenty-something."

"But I mean a really, really old man with a beard and a wig and almost blind."

She didn't say a word, but she looked up at the ceiling for about ten seconds, then she said, "Hmmm" for five more seconds, and then she said, "Let's talk to John."

She opened the office door and summoned John as if he was a valet. When he came, she said, "I noticed in one of your museum pamphlets, you occasionally put on little skits depicting one of the adventures of Sherlock Holmes. You wouldn't just happen to have a closet where costumes are kept, would you?"

Watson IV told her there was a closet in the hall outside the room where she and her mother were sleeping. She could help herself to whatever was in it.

"Thanks. Pete and I will be outside the back door ready to go to Buckingham in five minutes."

By the time I had gotten up to "the second storey," as they called it, she had found what she needed for my disguise—a wig, a beard, dark glasses, an old top hat, and a white cane. "Just put them on, Pete. I'll tidy you up on the way to Buckingham," as if I ever needed any tidying up. Then she darted into her bedroom in too much of a hurry to close the door behind her. When she came out a minute later, she was still tucking in her blouse.

To be honest, I seldom pay much attention to women's clothing unless someone draws my attention to it. A couple days earlier as we were waiting in the airport, Shirley said to me, "Doesn't Samantha look lovely in that new dress?" Of course she did, but if I said that, it might imply that she wasn't looking lovely when she was serving tables the previous day. So I thought it was usually best not to go overboard on comments about what a woman happened to be wearing. For all I knew, she might have been wearing the same thing for the past week.

But as we went down to the ground floor in the museum's lift, I had two questions to ask my valued accomplice: (1) "What's the plan?" And (2) "Are you sure you want to wear that grubby old blouse when we are visiting the Queen in Buckingham Palace?" That was probably not the most politically correct way of phrasing it, but octogenarians don't have time to worry about being politically correct.

"I'll explain everything on the way there," she answered calmly. "But, Pete, when we get out of the elevator—I mean, lift—I want you to walk alongside me through the dining room and between me and my mum, so she doesn't see this blouse. She would have a fit if she saw me dressed like this today."

Samantha leaned into me as we got out of the lift, which I didn't mind at all. Her mum and Mrs. Hudson were in the kitchen on my other side, which explained why Samantha had merged into me.

"Ta-ta, Mum, see ya later."

"Let me see how you look, Sammie," came the voice from the kitchen.

I answered quickly for Samantha, "Don't have time for that, Mum, Watson IV is waiting for us out back." I hope she didn't mind my calling her "Mum," even though that would imply that she was at least 110 years old.

Samantha almost carried me outside into Watson's auto. It wasn't large and I bumped my head as I got in, displacing my wig.

"It's OK, John. I'll take care of it. Let's get moving. Speed is more important than beauty."

Sometimes Samantha could be very eloquent.

In a moment we were driving down Baker Street, and Samantha was fixing me up, although I suppose the King's English (and no doubt the Queen's too) would be to say that she was neatening me up.

"What's your plan?" I asked again. I thought maybe she had forgotten that she was going to let me in on it.

"I don't have a plan," she answered and then smiled.

"If you don't, who does?"

"You do, Pete. All night long, I tossed and turned trying to think of a wild crazy scheme that the Queen would see as one of those daft American ideas that might actually work, but I couldn't come up with anything until your idea this morning."

"My idea this morning? I don't get it."

"It was brilliant, Pete, and it might actually work."

"What might actually work?"

"You playing the part of a blind old man, just shuffling along."

"Yeah, that might fool the reporters, but it doesn't help us find the Queen's brooch."

"It's a long shot, Pete, but it's the only card left in our deck."

Now I was confused. Was she playing the horses or playing poker? But there was no time for more questions now. We were inside the grounds of the palace and Watson IV left us off at the first sentry post.

We knew that Clarice didn't have much time to set it up for us, so we were pleased that the first sentry, after suspiciously looking us over, discovered that our names matched the names on his list, asked for further identification, and then waved us on to the second sentry. The second sentry took more time with us.

"Most unusual," he commented.

"But we just received the call from Clarice, telling us to come as quickly as possible."

The sentry shook his head, so I felt I needed to explain. "And she is the private secretary to the Queens' deputy priva— . . . or maybe she's the second private secretary to the assistant deputy queen."

He quickly picked up his phone to make sure we were legitimate. As soon as he finished his call, he said, "She is waiting for you inside the palace."

The only words Samantha said to me as we walked toward the palace were, "I hope she has a sense of humor."

And the first words Clarice uttered as she let us enter the palace were, "And you're presenting yourself to the Queen like that? I hope she doesn't take it as an insult to Her Majesty." She was quiet as she escorted us into the waiting room, and then she said, "This is all most unusual. She usually regards these early hours as her private time. Sometimes her favorite dorgis are with her for a half-hour or so."

This time there was no waiting to see the Queen. As soon as Clarice informed her that we had arrived, the little green light in the waiting room started blinking and we were ushered in.

Samantha curtsied. I think she must have been practicing, because if this were the Olympics I would have given her a 9.9 for this one. As for me, I did better too. No one commented about it, but it couldn't have been much worse.

The Queen seemed stiff; her features taut and strained. It was almost as if she were being carved on Mount Rushmore. For a long second or two, no one said anything, and I remembered from last time that I should not speak unless I was spoken too. It didn't look as if the Queen intended to speak to me at all this time.

Finally, she asked Samantha, "And what do you think you accomplished yesterday?"

"Nothing, your Majesty. We apologize for the publicity. We had no idea that terrorists were in the same area where we were searching for your brooch."

"That's the honest truth," I interjected, because I always thought that honest truth was the best kind of truth. I don't know if the Queen and Samantha agreed or disagreed about honest truth, but both of them turned and glared spears at me, and spear-glaring can be painful. After a few seconds of spear-glaring, the Queen continued.

"When the Sandringham terrorists were captured, they revealed that subsequent bombings were also planned for Holyrood Palace in Edinburgh and St.George's Palace in Windsor with similar explosives. But thanks to you, the terrorist plot has been exposed."

Both the Queen and Samantha were smiling now, and Samantha seemed to be relaxing a bit. She admitted, "But I would never have noticed the incendiary devices if we hadn't been looking for your brooch."

"And what are your plans for today?" The queen finally looked in my direction and seemed to be directing her question to me.

I hesitated to say anything. "We felt that you would be dismissing us from your royal service this morning, but just in case you didn't, Samantha had a plan." I looked at Samantha to continue because I didn't have a clue what the plan was.

The Queen clarified matters. "Yes, I was upset by all the publicity and I felt certain that you would involve the Queen in the matter, but as far as I can tell, you didn't."

"No, we didn't, your Majesty," Samantha assured her.

"Good. So then you are still on the case. But you must have an explanation for appearing before the Queen dressed as you are.'

I was going to explain but Samantha beat me to it. "The media took Pete's photo last night, and we thought it might appear in today's newspapers, so he needed a disguise or else the media would be tracking us wherever we went."

The Queen nodded. "If he weren't with you, I wouldn't have recognized him." Then she looked at Samantha. "And what about you? The other day you were dressed beautifully."

"Thank you." Samantha put her head down on her chest for a few seconds before looking at the Queen. "Well, I was sure that you would be dismissing us, and when you did, I had one last request."

"Yes?"

"That I could see one of your dorgis and perhaps even hold him for a minute."

The Queen smiled. "I certainly could let you see one of them, but they are very partial to me, and it would take a long time for any one of them to allow someone else to hold him. I'll show you what I mean." She rang for Clarice.

When Clarice appeared, she told her to open the door into the side room and allow one of the dorgis to enter.

The dorgi walked out slowly toward the Queen. Obviously, he had been well trained.

"This is Lord Nelson," the Queen introduced. "I name my dogs after famous British heroes."

Suddenly Lord Nelson ran to Samantha and almost knocked her over.

"Nelly, behave," the Queen commanded, but it did not do any good. "He responds better when you call him Nelly, than Lord Nelson."

"It's OK," Samantha said, reaching for a nearby chair so she could sit down and provide Lord Nelson with a lap. "This is why I wore this old blouse," she explained to the Queen. I call it my doggie blouse. I was hoping one of your dorgis would respond like this. Pete thinks that one of your dorgis— perhaps Nelly—could help us find your brooch. He also thinks that your brooch was lost in St. Paul's Cathedral. Don't you, Pete?"

"I do? Oh, yes, I do." I hated to be put on the spot like that. I think Samantha just enjoyed snuggling with Nelly and wanted to have a few more minutes of that pleasure before returning the dog to the Queen.

I had forgotten exactly why I had thought that St. Paul's was the likely spot for the Queen's brooch to be found. It had something to do with the fact that it was the last place on Samantha's list, but I didn't think the Queen would buy that as being a logical explanation. So I had to think quickly, and thinking quickly was not my specialty any more, if it ever was. "Well," I said, making the "well" as deep as possible. And if that weren't deep enough, I said "well" a second time, digging it even deeper, recalling everything I could about Anglican worship. "As you know, in America the Anglicans call themselves Episcopalians, and I have occasionally worshiped in an Episcopalian service in America. The thing that struck me most about the Episcopalian service was the amount of exercise that a worshiper gets. As a result there are probably more obese Presbyterians than Episcopalians. First of all, after you enter and prepare to slide into your pew, and incidentally, since you are the head of the church, you should consider changing the word pew to cushion or padded seat. You don't attract people to church when you say, 'Come to church and sit in your *pew.*'"

The queen didn't say anything, but Samantha was shaking her head and muttering, "Get on with it, Pete," so I did.

"But before you move into your particular pad, you do something you call a genuflect, which is sort of like the stance of a football lineman in America, touching his knee to the ground before he is ready to charge. And then you spend a lot of time kneeling, and in some of the better heeled churches they have kneeling pads, which I suppose were invented to make it easier on scrub women who spent every other day of the week on their knees. Of course, you have to stand from time to time to sing or pray. And sometimes when you stand you either kiss the person next to you with a holy kiss, or else twist around and pass the peace. At first, I didn't understand what it was a piece of. I was looking for a piece of pizza or something like that. But all told, there are plenty of calisthenics in an Anglican church, and if a brooch is going to fall off your dress, it would be more likely to fall off of it when you are doing sit-ups in an Anglican church than it would be when you are smelling flowers at a flower show or when you are bending over a hospital bed in the dedication of a new facility."

I amazed myself in how eloquent I could be when I really tried.

"That makes sense," said Queen Elizabeth, seemingly surprised that anything I said would make sense.

"Yes, it makes sense to me, too," said Samantha, doing another graceful curtsy. Now that she had learned to do a royal curtsy, she seemed to want to show off her skill. "And that is why we come to the last big request we make to your Royal Highness."

"And what is that, my dear?"

"St. Paul's is a very large, majestic cathedral, and it would take Pete and myself a long time to search through it and find your missing brooch. However, if we could borrow Nellie for a couple hours," she paused to stroke the pet again, "I am sure we could find the brooch quite quickly."

I raised my eyebrows as I looked at my partner. She had more confidence in the plan than I had.

"But," the Queen inserted, "the guards don't allow dogs in the cathedral."

"No, but if they are guide dogs, or as they are often called in the States, 'seeing eye-dogs,' they will be permitted to guide their masters."

The Queen looked back at me. I bent over further, pulled the dark glasses out of my pocket and hunched over my cane. I couldn't tell what she did next, but I heard her say, "This is highly unusual, but, Samantha, I have confidence in you. I see that you love dogs and it is obvious that Nellie enjoys you, so I am calling in Clarice, and I am writing a note, authorizing the release of Lord Nelson into your custody for four hours. In four hours I expect the return not only of Lord Nelson but also the diamond brooch."

I saw Samantha's broad smile followed by another curtsy toward the Queen while holding Lord Nelson in one arm. I wasn't sure if Samantha was smiling because she would be able to hold

Nellie for four more hours or if she really thought that the dog would lead us to the missing brooch. Or maybe she was smiling at her accomplishment of being able to curtsy and hold the dog at the same time.

CHAPTER 11

In the waiting room we phoned Watson IV and told him we were ready to be picked up. As we waited, Clarice was turning to ice again. At one point, she said, "I am not permitted to ask questions of the Queen's guests, but" and then she pursed her lips as if she had said too much already.

"What is it, Clarice?" Samantha asked, "We will tell you what we can."

"But, and I may be entirely wrong about you, but I think you are the biggest con artists who have ever had an audience with the Queen."

"Oh, no, Clarice, we are on a royal mission for the Queen. Aren't we, Pete?"

I don't know why she had to invite me into the conversation. She was doing very well by herself. But I nodded. And I tried to think of a comment that would impress the Assistant Secretary to the Queen's second vice- deputy adjutant (or whatever her title was today), and so I added, "Yes, it's a top secret enigmatic escapade for Her Loftyness." Samantha knew I had a way with words.

Clarice escorted us to the main entrance, and from there the three of us—Samantha, Nellie and I—walked to the first sentry post. Samantha was holding the leash and getting Nellie accustomed to her voice, while I kept a tight grasp on the permission sheet, signed and sealed by the Queen. One of the sentries said, "We have never before seen one of the queen's dorgis over here before."

Nellie had her long snout to the ground, sniffing the strange smells on this side of Buckingham. I wondered what would happen if Nellie broke away from Samantha and hightailed it onto a main thoroughfare.

Then I heard a shrill voice call my name, "Pete, come here." I turned around and saw Clarice in the entrance calling for me and motioning for me to come. I didn't why she was calling for me, but I ambled in her direction as quickly as I could. As I got closer, she said, "Pete, I have something for you."

"What is it?"

Before answering, she asked, "Do you know how to use it?"

She was giving me a rare smile now. "It is called the Royal Poopa Scoopa." She took special delight in giving me a task that fit my capabilities.

"I think Samantha will give me the necessary instructions," I answered. I folded the permission sheet and stuffed it in my pocket and then returned to Samantha with the Royal Poopa Scoopa. I just wish Samantha hadn't asked me the same question: "Do you know how to use it?" But she asked it with a different smile. At least I think it was different.

Before I had a chance to analyze the smiles, Roger pulled the car through the main gate to pick us up. He had apparently gotten back from his errand and was ready to resume his "day job" as the museum chauffeur.

Samantha and Nellie climbed into the front seat with Roger, while I contorted myself into the back seat with my Poopa Scoopa.

"What do we have here?" Roger asked Samantha.

"It's just a dorgi," she answered.

"People will ask where you got it."

"Like you, for instance?"

I had to butt in. "Roger, this is privileged information, but for your information, I have a paper in my pocket—somewhere, at least I think it's in one of my pockets, authorizing us to have it for four hours."

"What can you do with it for four hours, Pete?"

Samantha knew much more about what you can do with a dorgi in four hours than I would ever know, and she wisely answered, "That's privileged information, too, Roger." It was a good answer and I wish I had said it, but maybe I did and forgot. "By the way, Roger, this dorgi is not an 'it.' It's a 'he' with the name of Lord Nelson, and also by the way, Roger, we aren't going to the Sherlock Holmes Museum; we are going to St. Paul's Cathedral, if that's OK with you, Pete."

"Well, if you're going to St. Paul's, I'll have to turn back and take the Great Queen Street. It would have been nice to know that before I started." Roger was getting a little testy.

Lord Nelson was getting a little testy too, but Samantha kept talking to him and soon he was settled on her lap again. When all was quiet, I asked Samantha, "Do you think we'd have time to go to another place, if I'm all wrong."

"Pete, you can't be wrong. I thought you were convinced that St. Paul's was the place; at least you convinced me that you were convinced when we were talking to you-know-who."

"Yeah, I know, but now I'm starting to un-convince myself."

"Aw, Pete, this has got to be it."

"Yeah, but what if I'm wrong? I've been mistaken before, you know."

Roger tapped on the brakes, causing a yip from nervous Nellie. "And now you want me to drive you someplace else?" the chauffeur moaned.

"No, Roger, let's go to St. Paul's. Pete seldom makes mistakes, and he makes them only with women."

I couldn't let that go by unchallenged. "Oh, come on, Samantha, that's not true."

"What's not true? That you seldom make mistakes or that you only make them with women?"

"I haven't made any mistakes with Ariana yet."

"Yet!"

"Do you really think that she would want to take me to Paris?"

"I don't know for sure, but yes, I really think she would like you to take her to Paris."

"Let's forget about Ariana."

"You brought her up, Pete."

"And besides, she isn't my type."

"If you say so! You don't have to convince me, Pete; you have to convince yourself."

"Excuse me," interrupted Roger. "But who's Ariana?"

"Nobody important," I said quickly, hoping to end the discussion.

Samantha turned her head so I could see her raise her eyebrows.

Apparently that settled it for Roger. He informed us that we were passing a public parking area, but he would take us to the south entrance of St. Paul's to let us out. "But they won't let you take your dog in there. You may have to wait out on the sidewalk with Fido."

"Lord Nelson, if you please," Samantha corrected him.

"Whatever. Anyway, I will park and then I will wait outside for you. Probably one of you will still be outside with Lord Nelson and the Poopa Scoopa. By the way, when I talked on the phone a few minutes ago with John Watson, he said that the reporters were at the museum again. Apparently there was an incident near Trafalgar Square, and the police suspect terrorism."

"Oh, great," groused Samantha. "I thought we took care of that."

In front of St. Paul's, I got on my dark glasses and stepped gingerly out of the car. Samantha put the leash in my hand, and said, "Let me do all the talking." We left the Poopa Scoopa with Roger.

Nellie and I followed Samantha to the entrance. I didn't hear what she said at first, but I heard the guard's comment, "That is not a usual guide dog."

"No, it isn't. In fact, it is very unusual, and that is what makes him so very good."

I thought she was going to play her Lady Clydesdale role again, but she didn't need to. She showed her identification, and I reached in my pocket for my wallet, as she said quite loudly for the guard to hear, "It'll be OK, honey; they just want to make sure we aren't terrorists." She was a good actress.

I was bending at a sixty degree angle and I could see a bit over the top of my dark glasses, but Samantha gave me a guided tour anyway and said it loudly as if I were deaf as well as blind.

"This is awesome, Pete, I mean, Grandpa."

I whispered back to her. "They call this the nave."

She repeated in her guide-voice, "The nave is awesome, Grandpa."

We followed Nellie up the aisle, and several times Samantha would go to him and direct him to sniff the aisle, but Nellie didn't show signs of recognizing anything with the queen's aroma.

We had slowly made our way to the front. I whispered to Samantha, "Nellie seems to be pulling me forward."

"Good. That means she is onto something."

Just then, Roger tapped me on the back. "We need to talk."

Samantha joined us and whispered, "Talk to me, Roger, and Pete, you go ahead and follow Nellie."

Over the top of my glasses I could see we were at the second pew, and that's where Nellie stopped and gave a yip that reverberated around the great dome of St. Paul's. I was sure that St. Paul's had never heard anything like that yip. I sat down. Nellie was trying to get into the rack attached to the pew in front of us. It held a prayer book. I pulled out the prayer book, but there was nothing in it. Nellie was pawing the rack itself. Maybe there was something stuck to the bottom. I put in my hand and tried to reach, but my fingers were too stubby. Nellie was so excited, I feared she would let loose with another yip or yap.

I took off my dark glasses and saw Samantha and Roger slowly walking down the aisle. I motioned to her to come quickly.

When she got close, I whispered, "I think Nellie found it, but I can't reach it. See if you can do it."

She stuck her slender hand into the rack, and it was impossible for her to pull out whatever was lodged in it. Nellie could hardly contain herself. Now two guards had arrived. "You will have to take the dog outside. He is creating a disturbance."

"OK, Grandpa, let's take Nellie out. But Roger, you stay here until they get my jewelry out of the prayer book rack."

Sometimes it takes me a while to latch onto Samantha's brain waves, but this time I was with her. She knew that Nellie would have to leave the church, and that he wouldn't leave it with me, but she might be able to convince him. It wasn't easy because even as Samantha was walking out with him, Nellie kept looking back, and a couple times jumped up, threatening to pull away and go back inside the church. But eventually we got outside to a bench. All three of us needed the rest, although Nellie's nose was angled to the cathedral and if Samantha hadn't held him firmly, he would have dashed back in.

"Do you think that's it?"

"Nellie sure does."

That was about all we said for several minutes, although we said things like, "What's taking them so long?'

And then I asked about what Roger was in such a stew about.

"Oh, that. I think Roger still lives in an academic world. Every little problem seems to be a 9/11 experience to him."

"OK, so what was it this time?"

"He says the MI6 – whatever that is—wants us to leave the country in twenty-four hours."

"What's the rush?"

"John IV was told that we are on a terrorist hit list, but I find it hard to believe."

"Samantha, this is serious. MI6 is another name for the British secret intelligence service."

"You mean I won't be able to do any shopping with my mom?"

Before I could answer her question, Roger came out with one of the guards. Smiling broadly, he handed the diamond brooch to Samantha. "We had to take the entire rack off, and in the process the pew was damaged."

Then the guard took over. "So the pew will need to be replaced. And you will have to reimburse St. Paul's for it. I have some papers for you to sign, certifying that this was your brooch, and that it was because of your carelessness that the brooch was stuffed into the prayer book rack."

Samantha asked Roger to get the car, and then she turned her attention to the guard. "You see, sir, this brooch isn't exactly mine. It really belongs to an elderly friend. She is actually older than my grandfather here." When she pointed at me, I bent from a sixty degree angle to a forty-five degree angle. "She loves to worship here at St. Paul's, but because of her age, she can't come very often. She has dogs too, like my grandfather here. In fact, she lent my grandpa one of her favorites to help him today. Isn't that right, Grandpa Pete?"

The guard seemed to believe Samantha's explanation, but I thought I could add to it.

"If you have other questions, just ask my long-time doctor, John H. Watson IV at the Sherlock Holmes Museum."

"How long have you known Dr. Watson?"

"Let me see now." As I looked over my dark glasses, my mind went blank.

So Samantha tried to help me. "I think you said you knew his father and grandfather."

"Oh, yes, they were good old chaps. What were their names now?"

"I think you told me they were John Watson III and John Watson, Jr."

"How could I ever forget Junior? Must be the beginning stages of dementia."

"Or else," Samantha inserted quickly, "it's time for your nap."

Just then Nellie pulled at her leash, and Samantha responded, "Can you wait a minute, Nellie?"

Nellie couldn't wait, but found a lamp post that had been used for the same purpose previously.

"I'm sorry, sir, but you can contact Watson IV if you have further questions."

Fortunately, Roger was pulling in toward the curb as we were leaving the guard, so I could retrieve my Poopa Scoopa materials from the back seat of the car, do my assigned task, and get back in the car without wasting time. Samantha, who made friends with everyone, waved to the guard with a merry "Ta-ta."

CHAPTER 12

The first thing Samantha asked in the car was. "Roger, did you say twenty-four hours?"

"That's what John Watson told me."

"Then you have to take us to Buckingham first."

"I figured that. To return the dog."

"Yes, to return Nellie. When I get back to the States, I'm going to see if I can buy a dorgi."

"But, Samantha, you already have four dogs."

"You know, Pete? That's exactly what my husband will say."

"And what will you say?" Samantha sometimes had entire conversations worked out in her mind before they happened.

"And I will say, 'But a dorgi is different.'"

We were quiet for a while as Roger was navigating the streets of London. Then as there seemed to be a traffic lull, he said, "John Watson has booked three seats on a 10:30 flight tomorrow morning. Should get you home by late afternoon."

"Awesome."

"He has also phoned your contact woman at Buckingham—what's her name?'

"Clarice," Samantha offered.

"Yes, that's it."

And so at Buckingham, Clarice met us and ushered the three of us in, the three including Nellie, not Roger. We told the Queen what a marvelous dog Nellie had been.

Samantha didn't use the word marvelous; she said "awesome."

Nellie took her place on a footstool next to the Queen and within thirty seconds went to sleep. We told the Queen of the problem we had in extricating the brooch from the prayer book holder.

"And no one knows it is mine?" asked the Queen.

"Not even our driver, nor the guard at St. Paul's," I answered. "John Watson IV must have known that we were looking for something that one of the royalty at Buckingham felt was important, but he didn't know what it was nor why it was so crucial that someone from America should be called to find it."

She examined the brooch carefully to make sure it was the same one she had been given. Then she looked up at me. And at that moment I yawned.

Yes, I yawned. I needed a nap.

"I'm sorry, your Highness. I'm very sorry. I meant no disrespect."

She smiled at me. "I know you didn't. Sometimes octogenarians like us need our forty winks."

Then she reached to the side and pushed the button to summon Clarice.

When Clarice entered, the Queen said, "This fall, when we have the annual knighthood and ladyhood ceremonies, would you please add the names of Pete and Samantha to the list? American citizens are not usually considered for the honor, but if you don't mind and if you no longer are in the crosshairs of the terrorists, I think you are eminently qualified."

"Awesome," Samantha said, and gave a curtsy that you had to see to believe.

I bowed my head, and I don't know why but tears started flowing down my cheeks. It must have been that I was very tired.

ABOUT THE AUTHOR

Bill Petersen and his doppelganger William J. Petersen have written more than thirty books, including

Another Hand on Mine (McGraw Hill)
Those Curious New Cults (Keats)
25 Surprising Marriages (Baker)
Complete Book of Hymn Stories (Tyndale)
How to be a Saint while Lying Flat on Your Back (Zondervan) *
100 Amazing Answers to Prayer (Revell)*
World Changers (Masthof)*
100 Books that Changed the Century (Revell)*
One Year Book of Psalms (Tyndale)*
Christian Travelers Guide to the U.S.A. and Canada (Revell)*
Meet Me on the Mountain (Victor)
Martin Luther Had a Wife (Tyndale)
Jeremiah (Masthof)

And, of course,
The Octogenarian Sleuth Series:
       The Case of the Magic Telescope
       The Body in the Elevator
       Lucky and the Mafia

*Co-authored with people who knew what they were talking about.